Crossing The Kattegat

— Other Works by Chuck Miller

A Thousand Smiling Cretins
Hookah
Oxides
Thin Wire of Myself
Harvesters
From Oslo — a Journey
How in the Morning
Northern Fields
Carnival Story (video)
Dead Dog

(many of the poems in this volume appeared originally in the **River King Reader Supplement**)

Crossing The Kattegat

By CHUCK MILLER

Mica Press / 2001 / Madison

ALTERNATIVE CATALOGING IN PUBLICATION DATA

Miller, Chuck, 1939 — —
    Crossing the Kattegat. Madison, Wisconsin: Mica Press,
    Copyright © September 1, 2001
    Librarians' Choice Series #1
    1. American poetry -- 20th century. 2. Radical poetry,
    American -- 20th century. 3. Working class poetry.
    I. Title. II. Title: Kattegat Crossing. III. Mica Press.
    IV. Series.
811.54
ISBN   1-879461-17-X
All Rights Reserved

Volume is 6.25" X 9.50" perfect bound, with alkaline paper. The paper used in this publication meets the minimum requirements of American National Standards Institute for information sciences—permanence for printed library materials, ANSI Z39.48-1984

For book information:
sales@bookzen.com
http://www.bookzen.com/books2/187946117X.html

Librarians' Choice Series #1

Printed letterpress in Cloister typefaces by
Route 3 Press, Shooting Star Road, Anamosa, Iowa 52205

PRINTED
IN
U.S.A.

Cover design by Merilea, San Francisco & Joe Grant, Madison
Cover photo © by Greg Anderson, Madison

For Dave and Ann

— Table of Contents —

for Attila Joseph	15
we run in the new deep snow	18
There is the jackhammer	18
The photograph gave you a start	21
Listening to the Polsko rock station	23
that and so much else	25
Lisboa	27
Chinese Bus	29
Claudia	32
asshole you'll suck my tobacco dick	32
Slovensko	33
Dr. John	36
for Stuts and Tangela	37
breaking the ice	38
for Helle	39
you still have a pencil and paper	40
Trinec, Czech Republic	41
prairie myth	42
Nowy Targ	43
for Phil who jumped from the bridge	44
for Rebecca and Steve	45
and so we pass our days	46
for Joe	46
for Linda	48
Talking dogs	49
in far places	51
Night of Chess	52
sleepers	54
sneezing	55
Sundays	56
Previews of Coming Attractions	58
over and over again you see them at the pool	61
as though he were speaking in some Slavic perfective	63
for John Stack (1940-1998)	64
river at dawn	65
old jack	66
tree souls	67
Pozor	68
Time	69
unemployment office	70
food give-away	72
for Yoga Barbara	73

winter flies	74
Kant, Kyrgystan	75
slow learners	76
audience	77
roads and the night	77
Nerval	79
flight	79
metaphysical questions	80
reading your own poems again	81
American night	82
the trouble with most people	83
at night	84
we will live again	85
for Wanda	86
a hard row to hoe	88
blind alleys	90
insomnia	91
no recourse but re-course	92
Playing Again at 60	93
pass foto	94
they meant no harm	95
blind in one eye and can't see out of the other	97
Northern Manitoba	100
American Gridiron	103
global warming	105
Illinois	106
extra virgin	108
watching a little group on the square	109
an apartment in the city of the dead	110
for Grace	111
for my father	113
crossing the Kattegat	114
Dingleberry	117

— PUBLISHER'S NOTES —

CAN'T REMEMBER EXACTLY when I met Chuck Miller, but it was in Iowa City in the early 70s. I was publishing an underground newspaper, the **Prisoners' Digest International (PDI)** in the basement of my home at 505 South Lucas and, since we had eight bedrooms, had established a halfway house for ex-prisoners.

The collective that published **PDI** was about 50/50 excons and anti-war activists ranging in age from late teens to some older men who had had brushes with the law, looked us up and joined us for dinner and conversation.

Chuck had spent some time in a federal prison for a pot charge. Unlike a couple of excons who were living with us and attending the University of Iowa Writers' Workshop, Chuck had been accepted but soon found the elitist atmosphere more than he could tolerate. He left to devote his time to writing. It was about this time— the early 70s — that we met. However, it wasn't until my partner Sharlane and I returned to Iowa City with our daughter Charity that we became friends.

With increasing frequency, Chuck participated in readings. A person couldn't help but be impressed listening to him. He's a fine writer and reads beautifully. Not sure when we all started thinking of him as family. It just happened.

We learned how remarkable a teacher he was when he proposed offering a literature course and mentioned that our living room would be the perfect classroom for a couple of meetings each week. Since Chuck had told the Workshop to "stuff it," there wasn't any place on campus he could use even though he continued to take courses at the University and does to this day when he's in Iowa City. The course Chuck had put together was "Proletarian Writers of the Thirties." Sharlane and I joined the 20 or so students who had jumped at the chance to participate, even though it was a non-credit course.

Though Chuck has degrees in Mathematics, Physics, Chemistry, English, and a number of other subjects, he's rarely employed by a regular school system. On paper he looks great. In person he looks scruffy and has an attitude. He rarely gets past the second interview for the simple reason that he cannot tolerate pretense, rules that make no sense and directives from principals to buy new clothes.

PRINCIPALS: it's an odd word for the heads of schools who, frequently, have no principles when it comes to dealing with teachers and teaching. Chuck gets a lot of that. And since clothes from St. Vincent's cover as well as clothes from the Gap, such "principles" are, as he succinctly puts it, "BS."

As for his ability as a teacher, I have never sat in a classroom with a teacher more skillful at imparting information—and making that information sing—than Chuck.

Chuck's "Proletarian Writers of the Thirties" course introduced me to more writers whose books I keep and frequently return to than any one I know — with the possible exception of Sharlane. When she and Chuck get together I want to turn on the tape recorder.

Through that course Chuck and I met Meridel LeSueur and became friends with her. Because of that friendship she visited Iowa City a number of times. For a week a few years later, she and I visited six or seven of the major colleges in Iowa on what I dubbed "The Meridel LeSueur Iowa Tour."

One memorable night Chuck and I drove Meridel from St. Paul to Iowa City for a reading. We drove all night in an old gas hog that ran out of gas between Iowa City and North Liberty at 4 a.m. Meridel, always making the best of a bad situation, said no one had tried that ploy on her since she was a young woman. We sat and talked until someone stopped and took me to buy some gas.

On the trip down Meridel spoke about her friends and was amazed to discover that Chuck knew details about all of them. At one point she turned to me and said, "He knows all my old friends — even those who no one knows." Chuck is like that when it comes to teaching and writing — thorough.

Meridel had turned 83, and our friends Jerri McCombs and Stuart Meade created a great poster for that "83 and Ripening" reading. She drew one of the largest gatherings a poet ever attracted in Iowa City's Old Brick. Meridel was born in Murray, Iowa, and her peers came from all over the state to hear her that night.

Chuck and I joined the growing legions who loved Meridel. It was during those few days that Meridel had a chance to read some of Chuck's poetry. She not only admired his work, but loved his attitude as well. Said he was the best there was. And kept saying it until she died 12 years later.

One story she was particularly fond of was about Chuck filing a law suit against the University of Iowa. Seems a professor in the English Department had made a derogatory comment about Chuck in a lecture hall. He never paid much attention to such things, but the man made the mistake of trashing him and then trashing his poetry. Chuck's response was to tell him he could accept criticism from people who knew something about literature, but not from fools. He left the lecture hall, walked across the street, hired a young attorney and filed suit against the University for slander. He won, was awarded $15,000 and used it for an extended trip to the Scandinavian countries where he learned enough of the language to prowl the libraries doing research and reading about the writers he admired. He came back with another manuscript, and **From Oslo — A Journey** was published.

Since that time he has taught in Siberia, Yugoslavia, Czechoslovakia, Kyrgystan and is considering returning to Siberia as we go to press.

Chuck once wrote an essay about Meridel LeSueur for a literary section I produced for a Phoenix monthly. It's the most reproduced document on my BookZen web site. In it he wrote; "One thinks of the two most destructive elements in American literature in this century —commercialism and academicism — LeSueur has resisted both fiercely and gone her own way."

Chuck Miller has done so as well and continues to do so. He goes his own way. Carrying the torch I believe Meridel passed to him.

Last week, in Siberia, a driver took a wrong turn, and the ensuing crash broke Chuck's jaw in three places and banged him up a bit. So he's at home, doing well, and he hopefully is no longer the angry poet without a job. He's still out there without a three-piece suit, without a boss, choosing Siberia as "a destination for the ordinary mind." I know why. He's helped me learn what he already knew.

    Joe Grant
    September 1, 2001
    Madison, Wisconsin

Crossing The Kattegat

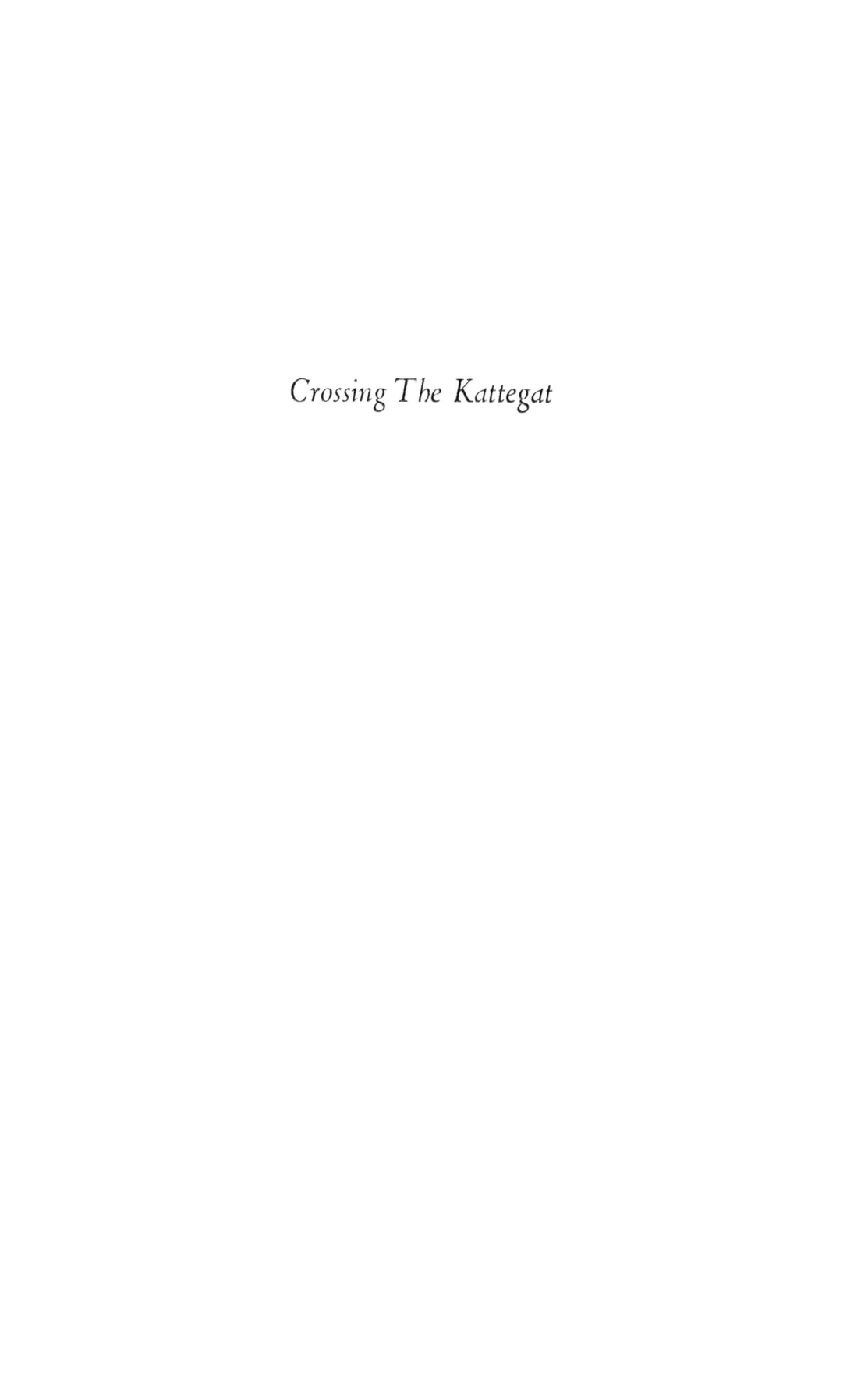

for Attila Joseph (for Joe)

leaving in the bleak winter dusk
from the Central Station in Budapest
leaving behind the cikan[1] gypsy families
huddled together and squawking noisily
the amputated man with only one leg
camping out in the little International Waiting Room
who when he finally turned toward you looked like yourself
you gave him your last ten Florints between you
even though you had to piss and that cost 10 Florints
having found, you thought, a little walkway to the basement level
on the outside of the station
where you could do it unnoticed for free
and yet as you turned from pissing
you became aware of an upper level passageway
from where people and therefore police and army men
who patrol the station, could have seen you . . .
and the International clerk charging us some fantastic fare
for our journey, even that now meaningless
cheated so often and in so many known and unknown ways . . .
out through the grids and multitudes of tracks
through the worn-out and decayed train yard
verging on neglected and rundown neighborhoods
the areas around the station where like a thousand Chicagos
poured together, a multitude of Clark Streets
and Dearborns jumbled into one
— little stray patches of weeds and overgrown places
which you take note of as possible locations to sleep in warmer
    months
past the dead standing Hungarian houses
different from any others you had seen
creating some unique sense in your mind
and truly you have never seen anything as desolate and beautiful
as this steely, purple-grey dusk

now coming to the marginal regions on the outskirts
always your favorites
making me think of your poem "Elegy" —
in the growing cold and dark in this nearby empty train
you wonder you begin to question to some shade
who is so close to you
so as to dream more consciously

when did you jump under Attila?
was it in the wan winter under the cold shining wheels
or in the summer with the smell and the dusky beauty of everything
too much to bear amid your suffering?
was it in front of the engine to be ground and cut up
under the locomotive beast bearing down on you?
or under the wheels of one of the cars?
the cars passing one after the other in terrible repetition
almost like some factory
and how were you dismembered, in what crumpling and rending
was your madness too dismembered?
your whole tormented life cut apart and healed there by death
or writhing still in little pieces and severed limbs
twitching with the residues of those insanities
was there one final lucid moment
or only a snuffing out a destroying away to nothingness?
but finally all these either/or posings too oversimplified
for the the strange death you were driven to

it must be cold Attila
riding there under the train
a presence, a ghost, a memory
it must be cold now after all these years
is this the puszta[2]?
the plain so much lyricized
so much like the prairie where I was born
and therefore for me so full of suggestive possibilities
Attila, the way they pronounced your name
as though the A was like a grunt of some initial bass tonality
and the ttila like some other lighter more musical word
in the National Center for Hungarian Literature
where they brought out the pictures of you and your family
as well as whatever English versions of your work
your slightly chunky lover, was she the one you bought
the grey blanket for in the poem?
and the critic who wrote that you did not deal
so much with images or metaphors
but with reality itself
it must be strange now being dead all these years
or perhaps not, only to me thinking about it
as we pass crumbling provincial rail stations
representing the abandonment of common love

I remember the trams of Budapest

that singing bird-like chirping of the electric wires
mixed with the ringing and scraping of the wheels
as we went down Bela Bartok Ulice[3]
toward neighborhoods with decayed houses and pungent back yards
so much more human than the central commercial district
where they had named a street after you
but only a street of banks and topless bars after all
I touched those photographs that must have been yours
and your family's
thus linking me by touch to you who left this world
two years before I was born
and the way the innocent young women librarians
seemed not to really know who you were
and barely knew your name
and yet showed me the materials on you
with such democratic and calm solicitude
as if were I interested actually
in this peculiar Hungarian postal clerk
why then yes they would help me discover something of him
and you would have had sympathy with this postal clerk after all
being the proletarian and communist that you were
and there is the Danube like a slate grey luminescence in the night
a river of fog, oh river remember
she cried, and yet did she expect
this transience to remember
what she herself might not?

Attila where have you gone now
so many years into the absolute
so many versts[4] down the Ugric[5] telegraph
down the trembling Madarsko[6] verbs which are so difficult to translate
you are with us still
your poems like live coals scattered in our hearts
and they strengthen us in our night journeys

[1]cikan: Roma or Romany
[2]puszta: plain
[3]ulice: street
[4]verst: a Russian measure of distance
[5]Ugric: a language family which includes Hungarian
[6]Madarsko: Czech word for Hungarian

We run in the new deep snow

we run in the new deep snow
because it is harder that way—
plunging down the precipitous inclines
struggling and beating up the hills

no, because if we continue
to run outside no matter

we know what it is like to be an animal
sinking in to certain depths
fleeing the hunters
it's the struggle of raising and lowering the legs
slipping and faltering
in the uneven footing
you sweat like a horse
running in this deep snow

to enter into this pristine pureness
like some strange being
half man half animal
drifting in the depths

and the skiers
who think you are crazy
they don't know

There is the jackhammer

there is the jackhammer
and the jackrabbit
and the antlered jackalope
to jack up in 4 different senses
to jack around as in i jacked around too much
and didn't get it done
jack-knife as a noun or a verb
remember all those stories about semis on icy roads
in so many words to bend in the middle
jack of all trades
all work . . . makes him a dull boy
with Jill went up the hill
or in playing jacks with a small rubber ball
and little jack stones that you had to sweep up with a grab

between bounces
or just plain car jack as in
"you mean we're out here on the throughway
and you don't have a blankin' jack"
or a nickname for John thinking of Ti Jean
"since i was packin my heater i threw down on him
jacked him up good too three c notes and a coupla sawbucks"
this common fellow
man or boy
maybe jack-tar the sailor or lumberjacks
or jack screw (as against its opposite)
any of the various machines used to lift, hoist or move
as in we are not unmoved
this male donkey or of jackass
standing for money as in do you have any
in romance or cards the jack of hearts
or in hunting this torch we carry
or light to attract game at night or fish
a small flag flown on our ship's prow
to show nationality (as in Union Jack)
and in electricity a plug-in receptacle
used to make "electric" contact
the male of some animals
or everyone as in every man jack of us no doubt sexist
to jack up prices or salaries
we know the former better than the latter
or never heard by me in colloquial speech (example of jack-up)
to reproach for misbehavior encouraged to duty
this sleeveless leather coat worn by medieval foot soldiers
or leather drinking mug
this large heavy fruit with tasteless pulp
and edible seeds
meaning large or strong jackboot for example
coming to above the knee
and we all know when we get it in the face
this jackal (yellow-grey meat-eating dog of Asia)
runs in packs does low dishonest work
this jackanapes of a high-grade simian
the jackdaw small crow-like bird but of equal raucousness
cold weather comin on as in Old Jack Frost gonna nip your bud
this grotesque little figure who springs up
when the lid is lifted on the box
this flower spike in its pulpit partly arched over by a hood

or the hangman of us all will ketch us yet
faery o'Lantern of shifting elusive light
this hollow bumpkin cut in the face
and when we finally hit it (or it hits us)
this pot of our dreams
sandpiper sniping at us from the beaches
these jack-straws we are attempting to remove
without upsetting the pile
this jack-string we hope
or hope not someone will pull
this strange every man word or woman syllable of us
ur-verb and catch name
from the Middle English Jacke or Jake
the Old French Jaque, Jaques
the Low Latin Jacobus Greek Ioakobos Hebrew Ya'aqob
this supplanter seizing us by the heel
the Spanish Jaco or Malaya Chakka
Turkish Chaqal Persian Shagal
Sanskrit S'rgala
all merging and shifting, evolving and descending
deriving in single strands or tangled
skeins but boiling down now
boiling away now to our so colloquial selves
we cunning linguists with our idiot idioms
betraying our true circumstances
and disjointed situations from whence our speech arises
our argot ridden locutions
and slang crooked and hardened expressions
to "i don't got nobody now so alls i do is jack off"
or "that politician jacks off and collects his money
but he ain't never done nothin fur me nor nobody i know"
or "listen man you're jacking me around every which way but loose"
and "after they lowered my wages and ripped-off my house
i didn't have jackshit left"
meaning none, nichts, or hardly any
this word which comes to tell the story
of our made-banal lives
speech current and verb murmur
this jacking back and forth
flux and assimilation
multiplying like jack rabbits
leaving us with this multiplicity of morphemic variation
ungraspable jet of air to designate
this crazy jumpword of our time Babel

The photograph gave you a start

the photograph gave you a start
he lay dead on the street flopped on his belly
an Indian with his face turned towards us
purple-black blood run out on the tiles
close beside him lay his "wooden gun"
that he had carved to take part in the uprising
a pocketknife tied on the end
they said . . . as a bayonet
but you couldn't quite make it out in the picture

either the tremendous courage
or the incredible foolishness
as your friend said for maybe a fraction of a second
the outline of he and his wooden gun
might have swayed some outcome
but what could he have been thinking
maybe there was a simple explanation
he and his friends might have discussed
the article said these Zapatistas
had embarrassed the Mexican government
their uprising coming as it did
just after the passage of NAFTA
as though the government
were some poor person we were to feel sorry for
the journalist seemed not to be interested
in what this Indian must have felt
to rise up against a modern army with a wooden gun
it was beyond words
was this Indian some fool
that we might have loved nonetheless
had we known him in everyday life?
or a helpless child?
yet there might be a strange way
in which his wooden gun did not misfire after all
for considering all the grotesque and useless deaths
we must digest each day
i couldn't seem to get over this one
even at such a great distance
that a human soul could be worth so little

are any of our souls then
worth more than the worthlessness of his?

21 —

yet so full of nobility or stupidity
rage or hopelessness
some mixture that is hard to grasp
still it plagues and puzzles
leaves me without words

should we then emulate this man
and begin to carve somehow our own wooden gun?
certainly not, something answers from inside
yes certainly, some greater sense replies
just a poor Indian from Chiapas
goes his way to death
we presume perhaps to judge him naif or foolish
if he could see into your life
he might have understood that your writing
is your wooden gun
and you even a greater fool
but with not as much courage

his wife
did she love him the more for it?
or only bewail the ungraspable sadness of his end
this absurd man with his absurd weapon
and yet perhaps no more absurd
than we ourselves

you want to cradle the poor son-of-a-bitch
in your useless arms
and weep for his hopeless death

Listening to the Polsko rock station

Listening to the Polsko rock station
remember Ghelderode, the Belgian writer
queried about rock and roll
"the final spasm in outer darkness," he said

you've heard Chinese
Czechoslovakian
and now Polish
—like a strange mutant fungoid growth on the original?
4th rate, 9th, 26th?
Or rather attempting to take it further
modifying for its own circumstances
or returning to some root sense
you can almost see the original bones
glowing and moving there in the darkness out your window
as this pained Polish voice nasalizes its angst
in an even more unintelligible rant
at least to you
than Czech, from which you might have picked up a word or two
well often enough you couldn't catch the words in English
anyway, could you?
then the Punks sometimes trashing out the vocals completely

you think of "The Secret Life of Plants"
where they recounted experiments of playing music for plants
and when they had to listen to a steady stream of rock
they died

yet you're from the 60's where they set out
to make it a real expression of our lives
and it was to whatever extent
(except that our lives were "radioactive"?)

then as it transpired boxed back into the commercial trap
shaped more and more by capitalism
selling us back distorted images of our struggle against it
or of giving in to its strangulating tentacles

but what of the Eastern bloc?
where it was more clearly an expression of revolt against tyranny
these questions you might ponder
and never quite answer

as your generation fades into age, obscurity and death
yet you know in your bones
that if there is not already
one day there will be a Mongolian rock
freezing the dust of the Gobi
and an Eskimo version disorienting the polar bears
—and you too involved marginally
in a strange parallel process

—now a patently false stylized voice identifies itself
as coming from Katowice
rocking transnationally
for the whole Beskydian region
jabbering con artist quick in some inhuman patter—

but then you remember thirty years ago
in Nuremburg
where earlier Nazis had their giant torch-lit parades,
in a rock club built on the ruins
some great bull of a man
but a priest yet
with his black suit and clerical collar
twisting some frail of a German fraulein[1]
scissoring back and forth
on the razor edge of their desire and torment
he the master and she the beautiful ragdoll
of his bidding
jerking her around as the saying goes
like some monstrous version
of the Devil jazzing the Virgin Mary
so intent on their reeling out and snapping back
somnabulist automatons on top a decayed wedding cake
you thought of Artaud and his Theatre of Cruelty
were these his "victims signalling through the flames"
or the persecutors of those victims
heating up what was most evil in themselves

---

[1]fraulein: young woman (German)

That and so much else

you know there's a falls there
a dam
well, i saw some fish
they had gone over the top
and now they were below it
they wanted back
maybe they had some brother
or a family of fish above it
they would try to jump back up the dam
but they couldn't make it
they would try though over and again
some of them till they died
well, i admired those fish, you see

i knew him from the library
every day he came to work on his mathematics
when we were tired or through with work
sometimes we would hang out
or with the few other library rats

it was night, the mathematician and i
had walked up the main road
to the bridge above the dam
we watched the silver sheen of the river
sliding over the spillway with intense force
we saw a fish
just a dark thing in the lace of the foam
struggling right at the lip
for a few seconds it seemed to be swimming in nothingness
suspended in the interstices between water and air
then it disappeared

he told me that on Sundays
he'd walk over and watch some fishermen
he didn't care for them
but he got a kick, it made him chuckle
when he'd see the fish get away
"he got out of the net, i saw it,
he was flipping and flopping to beat hell
and jumped right out"
his hilarity rose up into the night and toward the stars
"well, you see, it's like me and my theorem"

we walked back under the discolored sky
the high sodium lights casting a greenish-yellow spectrality
"men and fish are the same"
he worried for those that were caught
he knew what happened to them

a Palestinian, he was a Christian
one of the few, he thought it a kinder religion
the Muslims were too crazy, fanatic
his family had thrown him out for his beliefs
wife, children, lost to him
exiled, he lived in a cheap rooming house
with students half his age
all he had his work, his religion
a few friends, an old car
and his rooting for the fish,
myself, i thought the Christians and the Muslims were both crazy

i saw him again after i had gone away and come back
found him at the library
"and so how are you?"
and then "how are your fish?"

"yes, yes, the fucking fish," he said
starting to laugh
"i'm still rooting for them
maybe one day they'll make it
i say a prayer for them"—
with his ironic smile

Lisboa

it seems the music is coming from the ground
that puzzles you
then you find the stairs and the power of it pulls you in
down the stairwell and along the passageway
more and more intense as you follow round the bend
as if approaching some incredible source, a buried calliope
or some music the earth is playing for itself
there he is finally
a blind accordionist
sitting on a little folding chair
in a tunnel off Avenue de la Republic
grey head bent down and obliquely turned aside
as if a kind of shamed sadness or distance from his own music
as though hearing it in some other dimension
or so far within himself . . .
the sound sears into you
as if you had ears in your breast
the bass under the crying treble
pours himself into it in long bitter squeezes
and aching pullings apart
one shoulder hunched a little lower
dragging out the songs
from his box of folding dreams
there's an undertone nothing so much as a dissonance
and sad
groaning and wooden
in even the gayer songs
that seem to roll out in a slightly drunken procession
staggering a little in their footsteps
blaring out suddenly in some Bulgarian contra alto
as the notes sheer against one another
some darker resonance
then gradually resume their dance-like air

you are transfixed
remembering drunken Finnish accordionists in obscure bars
playing with their dragspel [1]
the lugubrious half-Ugric obligatoes
for a few intoxicated pulp workers
and their scraggly working-class molls
as they tried to honky-tonk in a last-ditch dead end
of their carcasses' remains

your father bringing out his box from the closet
when you were a child
and playing with his crippled, claw-like hand
in that jerky country style
the old songs from his immigrant youth
for a moment the jesting and turning dancers came alive
then fading as if some other self were dying away within him
only to suddenly spring to life again
as with his powerful hands—he seemed to wake from sleep
he forced the bellows
struck a jarring harmony
and with those figures began to dance again
with a crude mockery and mirth
in a memory that only he could see

you think of the Czechs as he lights into a rollicking one
one of their native songs—a bitter love ballad [2]
something like " . . . you shit on my love
and have wasted my life"
the Americans stole it
changed it to:
"roll out the barrel
we'll have a barrel of fun"

you look for his money box or hat on the ground
and finding none you think
ah, playing for free, for the love of it
but then as you watch
the Portuguese come up and place a coin
in a little box connected to
and on top of the accordion itself
and they do not stint him
you think "before some boys
must have stolen his hat with the money
and now he has an almost fool-proof method"
but all you have are a few Swedish crowns
of no use to him
he pumps out Portuguese laments
for the expressionless Lisboans
until they turn and carefully place a coin in his box
and you watch his shut blind eyes
as he strains to get it just right
you wonder, is he only remembering
or does he still experience—

when he finishes
he stops abruptly with an expression of disgust and fatigue
breaking off what had been built up
with an air of abandonment
as though he couldn't bear to go on
although it was only morning
but then in a few moments
sits down on his folding chair once more
with a grim look begins to draw out
these echoes from the harbours of our souls
elucidating these tongues of fire
this beautiful grinding and droning
the awful shuddering and holding
in a cross-stitching of ivory and bellows
in a voice that cries out
when the other voice has fallen silent

[1]dragspel: accordion (Svensk)
[2]"Sko Laska": "Lost Love" (the name of this bitter Czech ballad)

Chinese Bus

it starts with a jolt
the ticket-taker's got to keep her balance, right herself
then it's bumpity-bump swerve
as she weaves through the crowd you see her swaying against the lurch
thumbing a little moisture off her foam pad
so she can finger one-two-three tickets
for the one mao[1] payment
same as one jiao [2]
a few hang back rather not pay at all
a few jiaos a day add up
today she hunts them down
pushing through the hard-packed passengers
but perhaps some other day she'll let a few off the hook
though eyeing them from time to time
through the forest of people
trying to make them guilty
or frightened enough to cough up
you know that i know who you are . . . now give it up
but what if an inspector's watching
when she lets a few slackers pass?
as well, she's got to open the doors at stops
sometimes one set won't open

then the people jammed at the front exit
will have to push their way all the way to the back
pushing and shoving
not only because they have to
through the sardine packed riders
but because they've learned to enjoy pushing and shoving
they'll lay waste with minor skirmishes and fights breaking out
she'll have to try to sort them out
frequently the passengers talk back to her
she'll have to give them a piece of her mind
or chuck a few off bodily with the driver
or a few of those public order keepers with the red armbands
the driver's got a kind of small gear shift
that she's got to adjust and fiddle with
as well as the larger one, she's always shifting down
or up, but also turning off the key and coasting
saving gas
and then she starts it up again, popping the clutch
you watch fascinated and amazed
as she works those gears and levers, shifts and pedals
clutching with her left foot, braking with her right
pulling the big black wheel around (taped over at the center
so she can grab it)
only a frail middle-sized Chinese woman after all
moving that gear shift from first to second
and on up and back down
constantly swerving around bicyclists
then having to swerve back in to avoid some big truck
or other bus
and her, right at the cutting front corner
if she doesn't swerve soon enough . . .
constantly crowding the bicyclists over to the side
in her face you see the strain deep-set
wearing her down bit
by bit
occasionally she'll make a half-audible remark
to the ticket-taker
communicate only a few words
it's as though they already know
what the other is going to say
and it goes this way
hour after hour
day by day

year after year
the old plodding bus elbowing into traffic
roaring along in some low gear

at the end of the shift
when they pull into the terminal
what results obtained?
the old labor and grind
the familiar fatigue

and at night
most of the time they drive with no lights
relying on the streetlamps
like a bus of the dead
going to the other world
you can't see their faces anymore
only vague darkened human presences
not so packed now
they can relax
and actually sit in the seats
the headlights will flick on only for a second
as though they are dreaming
in their nightmaze sleep
and when the bus of the dead
pulls up to the stop,
you feel an instinctual uneasiness
who are these . . . ?
and the driver maybe tired old Charon
ferrying them across
only a few more stops
they will be at the place where the dead get out

---

[1]mao: formal term for 1/10th of a yuan, the currency denomination in China (Mandarin Chinese)
[2]jiao: informal term for 1/10th of a Chinese yuan

Claudia

others will come after us
thronging these cold streets,
but warmed by some old love and grief
we already knew—
you slipped away
like your mama to an early death
no more to mourn

what sense
this senseless life
which carried you like a worn-out leaf
to your end?
we do not know, but only grieve

asshole you'll suck my tobacco dick

asshole you'll suck my tobacco dick
your whole life
pale white spectre
of a real dick
smoke bleeding between your lips
I'll come into your mouth forever
with poison jism and black tar
with jackboots of advertisers, laws, respectability
I'll step up and force my dick
into the mouths of your children
you'll watch mute
your heart cut out
for when they become dicksuckers early
I've got them by the throat
you'll see them on street corners lighting up
indifferent, blase
dead already and dead again, without knowing
sucking that grisly dick, mine
breathing its vapors
I'll eat out their lungs, heart and arteries
forcing them to suck me off
reach in with claw-hands of profit
rip out their breasts
their life ebbing away day by day
make it illegal to suck
any other kind of dick

human or leaf bud
send them to the penitentiary
for sucking any other dick than mine
with my Marlboro men and Joe Camels
we'll make it seem brave
to belong to the dick-sucking society
to give your life to death and dicksuck
even women "you've come a long way baby"
will suck me off openly
and with relish
toxic cum oozing out their mouths,
I'll stand shoulder to shoulder with the leading citizens
for the rich know
there are only two kinds of people
the masters
and the slaves

in the end
when my dick has been in their mouths for years
and they've sucked it dry of its cancerous juices
they'll beg me
on their death beds
for one last suck
on my long and terrible dick
before I kill them
and cum into their gape-holes forever

Slovensko[1]

the little obcerstvenies [2]
they have in the rail stations
you eat standing up
at the high tables
huddled over yourself
in from the bitter weathers

polevka [3]
or a plain meat dish with chleb [4]
only travelers
or the lowest of the low
frequent them
sometimes a kind of lulling peace and anonymity

struggling by in the dense crowd
a man with no arms
long haunted sleeves swinging useless
another lurching and waddling
his legs made to different lengths you see
by some industrial process
strapped in to the great clunking shoes of the lamed

the Sunday drinkers
having a stiff one
a big glass of pivo [5] or some slivowitz [6]
to make it through
the barren wastes of the day
the older women who serve up the food
no longer illusioned
move with a certain softness
worn-out Gypsies under the pale lights of dusk
a look of soiled and hopeless experience

sometimes the prostitutes would come on
one with dirt caked on her face
mumbles a sex coo
another humorous and friendly
goes back for the bread you forgot with your soup
brings it over dark eyes flashing
maybe cikan[7] you think
but after you give her a heel
which she eats, "dobre" [8]
she feels your pants, sensing a bulge
but instead finds a little jar of honey
you have stuffed into your pocket while moving
she becomes a human vacuum cleaner
trying to suck everything from your pockets
but still the only one
"schade" [9]
to suggest a little "Lublya"[10]
with some warmth and savour
false though it probably was

the drunks with open hearts
who would make some passionate
rigamarole of speech
the intimate revelations
of their thought and intoxications

shake your hand because you had listened to them
but only vaguely intimating some instinct
that might have moved behind their words
mutter "do Videnia"[11] with them to seal what had passed

night, the trains come in from the dark
the thick, tired men wearing old blackened overcoats
look up from their plates and a deep solitude
from where they come? and where they go?

someone in the corner behind you
knocking one back and getting hammered
you are there with them
the radiator clunks
and croaks in this fogged-in dream
like the strokes of a doomed bell
pick up your bag
shoulder it
recommence
this journey
to the end of night

[1]Slovensko: Slovakia (Slovak)
[2]obcerstvenie: greasy spoon diner
[3]polevka: soup (Slovak)
[4]chleb: bread (Slovak)
[5]pivo: beer (Slovak)
[6]slivowitz: hard liquor (plum brandy)
[7]cikan: Gypsy (Slovak)
[8]dobre: good (Slovak)
[9]schade: an expression of regret (German)
[10]Lublya: love (Russian)
[11]do Videnia: till we meet again (Slovak)

Dr. John

somewhere you had a few readers
one you remember as you walk the streets
of his old city
Dr. John from Alabama
you never knew how he got up here in the north
nor why they called him Doc
except maybe that he prescribed his own medicines
and plenty of them
he had given up on everyone
except you and the Russians
whom he read over and again

he seemed kind and intelligent
for the brief time you knew him
but you never saw him drunk
a mean one they said
and a troublemaker

hermit
intellectual
clown
convict
that is sentenced for life
to this aborted planet

cancer it was finally got him
now already gone for some years
he had lived in a little house
in the woods
just beyond the edge of town

what still remained of his accent
his soulful conversations and chronic laughter
his pixie poking of fun

who might remember him
you only know a few
now maybe he's drifted in the snow
on the drafts of wind
or up the mountain in the earth
"do the dead jump around
or climb mountains?"
he might have joked sardonically
giving it a piquancy with a twisted grin

for Stuts and Tangela

she made love to him
at the edge of a school playground
just as school was letting out
you thought of those dusky, balmy spring twilights after a rain
her generous and open lying with him
in the days when life opened—
and things were given away for free

not measuring so carefully or with such tremendous scrutiny
as they did before and now in this later era
but laughing with a twinkle in her eye
and a swing to her ass
nor what she would be called then, or later

and if some of the chldren stumbled on them
in the little break of trees
if this secret
had not been distorted in them already
that each of them came from such an act as this
and if they were not all bad
then perhaps this also might be worth something
they might have an inkling
of this lavish bestowal
as she urged him
"Paul, give to me . . . Paul"

breaking the ice

bicycling this early morn
out from Trinec
toward Horni Listnu and the Polish border
this time you have your Ausweis [1]
to find at the end of a tiny village
the road ends—
or becomes a cow path
before it can continue
to the next village with gold Russian-like steepled church
that caught your eye,
after following the path up a muddy hill
past a peasant woman trudging down
eyes me suspiciously
till it dissolves in a pasture
i try the other fork, past her again
gabbing with a neighbor
to find in another kilometer—dead end
in a hilled cluster of their greyshaded concrete-block houses
and a German shepherd barking gutturally
and writhing on his chain to get at me

from the hill
i can look back on the city
and it almost seems as if it had been bombed
from the columns and scarves of smoke
the massive cloud of debris that coils slowly upward
and disperses over all and sundry
coming back, it occurs to me
that since this is the border
no doubt they broke off the road
between the two villages, Polsko and Cesky
a quarter mile apart
to cut down on the border stations they would need
not to let anyone cross unprocessed or unheeded
neighbor to converse with neighbor without their permission
this absurdity and obscenity dawning on me
i pass her one last time, coasting now easily
and she lets go in her Polish or Czech
can't tell which
but the language of abuse being universal—
a virago spewing some territorial aggression
no better than the dog, or worse

but i'm quick to fling back as i pass
a "mother-fucking asshole" or such
and it's almost a relief
breaking the old ice
she standing for the countless many in this country or that
who begrudge your existence in their ethnic stomping ground
and you, solitary voyageur
who, traveling over this wasted earth
need no permission
from those who stain and soil it

  [1]Ausweis: passport (German)

for Helle

certain few women are blown your way
and perhaps they are among the best
not hard in the manner of speaking
yet they seem to know everything already
beyond your fumbling mortal sense

if you had some diamond drill-bit of instinct
to drive home in them
perhaps you'd yet strike love
deep in the wedges of their forged suffering
in the metallic alloys
of their disillusioned bones

but your only driller
some poor cock flesh and imagination
foolish and vagrant
ignorant babbler akin to its owner

and so you see them drift toward some better companion
or Arctic night of solitude
for which they summon their steel and level-headed courage

you still have a pencil and paper

you still have a pencil and paper
don't you?
there's time to write your way out
isn't there?
of these predicaments
that seem to shift one into the other
like abscesses opening

the collective becoming even more degraded
to assume that you'll make an individual solution—
dubious
but it might be the only thing in the end

as though having untwisted yourself this far—
new kinks nonetheless always showing up in the thought stream

or not even with the scribbling machines
finally just to think and feel
but now with the "power outages"
and the "model" becoming more than a little outdated
you'll have to go on with this
"antique receiver and decoder"
until the end—whichever comes first

with brief notes off the back of the boat

but still lay it down
as you can
the hammer-heads of the typewriter striker
rising up and inscribing
in our hopeful bronze

as good as it gets, they joke
taking the idiom from some scene
in the most debased medium
"shitspeak" we could call it

to insist still
in our better moments
that perhaps we could speak
or write in such a way
to articulate what seems most real
and make it stick

Trinec, Czech Republic

coming through the trees
in the late afternoon
coming home from work
from school
for you the same
as though you had never done with being a student
hear the water susurrating in the stream
awaken to the melting of the snow
and that transparent, intense, deep movement of fluidity
that will flow through you forever
reminding—
look about
as though something were missing

and then in the deeper forest
that soughing and soughing
—set off against an emptiness
as though the soughing maybe slowing
were also tired
in the wan late winter afternoon
were also alone
but no
only sighing that deep sigh
that deep still murmur of death
in the green density
brushing the boughs with its speech
playing over them
yet indivisible

coming out of the forest
you examine everything again
the broken ice, dirty snow
the small patches of ground
you feel what is missing
that other voice
a human connection
and you see you have come on some kind of death again
or disconnection
you have stumbled on it once more
as though following a siding

then the landscape opens out to a plain

sloping down toward the great steel factory
a bare winter plain
and you come upon some others
attempting their vacant evening errands
in their tired threadbare trudging
scrunching through the greying snow
the houses and the earth seem to gape at you
to gape open with a shrug and a faded light
well—?
then you are at your rooming house
the blowing dies away
the gate creaks strangely as you open it
as though to indicate what a skeleton
what an Ichabod Crane
you have become
enter your room realizing how you must think it all out again
stare into the darkness once more

prairie myth

night-scented spirit
girl of prairies
one day i'll double back
to that fly by lost night
and by the wind grieved village
rocketing along the rails
like a stained-glass freight train
jingling and shuddering
huffing and rumbling
racketing across green fields
glinting the sun into a weary cinder
making music as though my whistly steam engine
were a circusy calliope

approach that cornucopia Sphinx figure
in the midst of August ripe grainfields
silvery, naked
legs spread boomerang apart
train steam-puffing closer and closer to that tunnel
under the foliage and into the dark straight
across the dim inner being lit by breast-shafts Cathedralesque
through two small holes in the near top blue-bright sky
all this grain elevator of Illinois summers

and through, strangely returned to the past
an "our town"
their town that was never really ours

you stand slim and quiet
true to the spirit of place
but trembling and pregnant with uncertainty
and i, shadowy mosaic hobo
slipping off along old abandoned farm roads
disappearing in burning russet-hazy evenings fall
and you follow

we shall blow one long harlequin-strident blast
upon the stain-glass calliope of our souls—we're off!
racketing across green twilit fields
past rail crossings of their dim unknowing
and goodbye forever
modulate to the click of the rails
drift into night
becoming moaning wind
through night's corn patches
lost then finally
   among the smokes
      of leaves
         and griefs tempestuous
           and never
              never
                 see the Grandma
                        of your small-town earth again

Nowy Targ[1]

the silence of the woods
almost cures
the silence of the people

[1] Nowy Targ: name of a town in Poland

for Phil who jumped from the bridge

some mornings
we come up
like a heavy object being lifted by a crane
from a hole in the ground

some mornings
think of the obstacles in the way of life
even put there by life itself
or by your fellow human beings
to some human life
to most lives
to his
your good friend

at certain economic latitudes
certain longitudes of hope

more and more like a rain of meteorites
but, lest you exaggerate
watch them once more
navigating slantwise through a barren hail of stones
—what's called surviving
perhaps put in to port

but so many
so many founder
they go under
they go down in the deep
and perhaps know then best of all
what the rest
are trying to keep from knowing

for Rebecca and Steve

emus or ostriches
we didn't know which
they walked toward us with the same hinged movements as humans
but even more delicately
i supposed the more distinctly plumaged one
with the red beak and lips
was the male, but
why shouldn't it have been the other way around
if they were like us
they didn't seem frightened or agitated
as we stood only a fence away
but rather calm and thoughtful
nor did they seem to be looking for a tasty handout
we hung out together for awhile
their eyes so fantastically big
you thought they must have had a vision
of things somewhere along the line
not seeming to blink as they stared intently at you
but something would flash in the pupil
like a camera-shutter tripping
they seemed at just the right angle
to see both binocularly
but also from each side singularly, if they choose
their legs like the legs of knobby old crones
until the upper thigh which seemed thick and powerful
their heads so small, and maybe brains too
but you thought perhaps micro-chip wired
reminding you of giraffes somehow
had birds and horses once fucked
in a wild confusion of hooves and feathers
we spoke a few words to them
and they seemed to understand
when they ran
it was with a long graceful stride
their necks and heads like periscopes stuck up into a different reality
ah, those emus
our brothers
our aunts
we had encountered them
and they were ours
we were theirs

and so we pass our days

it's only a tempest in a teapot
ah but wait,
my tempest!
my teapot!

for Joe

maybe it was the ferns
whose delicate frondescent density a green inweaving
and which were always pictured in prehistoric times as giant
and coexisting with the dinosaurs
or the explanation which told that the redwoods had existed
during their times
and that some still now lived to be 2000 years old
of the quote from Steinbeck that
"even the most irreverent of men
fell silent in their presence"
and you thought no, now the most irreverent of men
would not fall silent
but when entering the forest
you were struck
was it the creaking, lapping, murmuring
of the clear stream
which first on one side, then on the other
or that the trail was made by the CCC[1]
which you always thought was a good idea
and being unemployed you could have signed right up for
the deep shade of the woods
the immensity of the trees
are you a worshipper of giantism?
the trilling of the birds in the openings
or mysterious glens
the peculiar red color of the cut or broken-off wood
some old smoldering darkened red like discolored brick
the crashed trees now lying on their sides
almost like elongated boxcars
sometimes with earth across the horizontal planes of them
growing plants, weeds
the toppled trees bowering the path
or acting as a bridge over the stream
remembering Hesse's "Glass Bead Game"
that this might be the forest equivalent

the old bikku said he was retiring to—
to put aside stories and pictures forever

or that you and your friend were the first ones up
and in to the wood
you grasped that you had to walk very slowly
slightly slower even than ambling
or then jumping down beside the stream
like a teenager full of bravado
drank from it and found it good
the silence when you stopped
except for the faint hum of the birds and insects
in the presence of the great-lived longevity
hoary speechlessness
or the roots naked of the fallen ones
like thinking bones of the inconceivable head
the thought that your father made it to Seattle once
hitch-hiking on the bum
and your mother to L.A.
but they had probably never seen anything quite like this
and in their last creepings and staggerings
might be moved by this wood
the story that a family had lived
in the burned, hollowed-out portion of one
during the depression of the 30's
the five-fingered, lady, or sword-ferns
all you saw, ferns in general
or that the Chinese had their own "dawn Redwoods"
Metasequoia Glyptroboides
that no one had mentioned when you were there
north of Harbin up in Manchuria?
where you had always wanted to go
someone told you
that the most beautiful women lived there
a mixture of Han Chinese and White Russian
who had fled after the Revolution
the thought that of the many things you see and experience
one will stick with you
of the thousand accidents of time and space
that speak to you
and enter in to you
and might stay with you till the end

[1]CCC: Civilian Conservation Corps

for Linda

        they called her chink
          or nigger chink
           red nigger
           yellow nigger

for the blacks she was not black enough
    the whites not white enough
  for the poor white and poor black trash
    too smart
  the girl gangs chased her
    the boy gangs might have raped her
  they both beat her
    she tried leaving school early to race home
  but some of the teachers would not let her leave
  5 minutes before the bell
although they knew her terror

these years later you tell me your story
    and the table between us
        becomes a long perspective

in your animated face
    i see Chinese-Mongolian cheekbones
        descending through your Indian ancestors
    the black slave brought from Afric
        in a torture chamber at sea

i cannot help remembering
    how the English expropriated the potatoes
    in the great famine
    probably starving the grandmother of your Irish grandmother

    all these sad and exploited strains
        mixing to create the woman of color
           which is you

  it pains me deep
    how they hated and tormented you
  i have no mercy on them
in my imagination i go back
    and beat them into bloody ribbons of flesh
        i do not care that they were children

      you rise up before me
          like a swirling of possibilities
a triangulation of hopes and affections
     in your face there is still the fragile child
        to whom they gave no quarter

     you and i will exist perhaps
     only for an extended moment
before the crusts shift
       some schism of alienation
           or desire
             parts us like floes breaking off
                drifting out
                    in the spring thaw

but in this moment
i clasp the girl of flowing colors to me
clasp the girl of red-yellow autumn lights and winter **darknesses**
look into your sad eyes
redeem them
for as long as our poor memories can grasp

Talking dogs

Gelsomina: why is Zampano the way he is?
the fool: if a dog could speak, it would
instead it barks

                                  — *La Strada*

they say some are cat people
others dog
you and your old lovers
always had dogs

they would enter in
to the various family conversations
speaking according to your ventriloquistic skills
sly comedians, philosophers, jostling siblings
you and your girl friends
sometimes giving them cross gender voices
bitching, so to speak
and kibbitzing

gradually the dogs were killed or died off
moondog

winnie
schiz
goo
sonny
life a long road
along which are strewn many dead dogs

and the women go their various ways
down the dusty path
and you yours
barely distinguishable in the darkness

one foot in the grave
the other on a banana peel
you find a new lover after a long dry spell
kind, intelligent
wholly wonderful
why she chose you
you don't quite grasp
it must be
that love is blind

as well she has a good dog, tipper
and again we are playing at
talking dogs, all the dog need do
is provide the body language
for us to improvise on

and then listen and understand
their various speeches
in order to move further along
in the dialogic discourse
"you'd watch out Miller
if you know what's good for you
all that smooching with my ma
horning in on my territory
I'll take a bite right out of your ass"

one day in the future
you never know when
we might bust up
or the dog die
maybe one of us

after we are all gone
or split apart
perhaps there will be one dog left
speaking for us all
only partially imaginary
this last dog
listening for her master's voice
but talking on and on
into the fog and sea rush
the last talking dog

in far places

in far places
i watch for your face
—look for you now
along the road

in distant cities
i seek you out amongst groups of blacks
amidst the archipelagoes
of the dream

in the face
of black children
i look for your innocence
for your childlike and smiling face

along the jostling streets
of strange cities
at strange depths
i search for you among people of color
angry or despairing
i will never know or understand

but you—
you are never there

A Night of Chess (for Mike)

I pound away on Giuoco's piano
making a few good melodies and harmonic changes
your game steadily improves
no longer frittering away your opening moves
neglecting to develop
but in the end you start up again
with quixotic attacks from the balcony

a series of hard-fought draws
giving me some deep satisfaction and equanimity
perhaps making us equal in our quest
the night hours steam open
joking at the frustrating twists and sharp countermoves
this game, obsessional, no doubt a bit weird
hunched over this thinking board
almost a kind of situational mathematics without numbers
yet in the long quiet pauses
a flickering of the invisible
resembling on rare occasions some meditational state

they can't take this away from us
the mind expanding in a struggle of naked thought
two humans alone in a bare room
a deep inner joy extracted from us
matching abstract possibilities one against the other
why it's almost better than poetry, less pretense
nothing to show for it except the experience itself
and the sharp challenge humming inside you

you speak of the history of it, the Malay and Parsi game
the variation in the pieces and rules
how it occurred to you to consider a new mathematical way
for evaluating the worth of various pieces
based on the squares of sweep or pieces jumped

we reach a point in the early morning hours
where our thought becomes somewhat phantasmal and unclear
claiming that each game, one after the other
will be the last
while pondering the situation i occasionally lose track
of whose move it is
each trying to finish on a note of clarity and lucidity
in the the empty fumes of early morning

some bleak but humorous seeing comes over us
a cascade of ironic twists and reversals
queer freakish games like mutant children
that one still loves and takes delight in
the stranger the better at this point

we invent a new variation
based on an impacted end game where neither of us
can hardly afford to move, a dense thicket of pitfalls
the game becomes a kind of surrealist time piece
of minor and oblique ticks
wheels turning one latch at a time
only then at a certain point to reverse direction . . .
namely that a player can simply pass by his turn
seemingly absurd in a game
where white always has the advantage by starting first
and this only by a bare move
yet this abstention strangely sense-making in chess as in life
we speculate as to the number of times
a player might actually avail himself of this arcane privilege
ruin the stale-mate perhaps
but if each player would in turn pass . . .
the fifty-move draw become the fifty-pass draw
only signified by a flick of the eye
or a brief nod of the head
but if on the third, tenth, thirty-seventh
or at last forty-ninth turn
a player might then choose to move . . .

dawn and we are finally kaput
you go home in the morning fog
past blocks that appear like broken-off chess pieces
under the oaks that in the mist
might or might not exist

yet breaking camp there remains a good residue
as i fall asleep
i think of the old Chinese men
bent over their own version
a crowd of silent onlookers gathered round
here and there along the roads and dusty byways
brothers of the long thought
the sly and humorous twists . . .

sleepers

the special ones forming themselves out there
unbeknownst in the depths
your children let not play tag
with the waves
for the sleepers . . .
their crests rising higher
you can almost see them
when you close your sun-drenched eyes
the green quartz of them
—knock you down and the undertow drag out
beware the sleepers
walking bare in the surf
—the sea more than enemy enough

the sun on its changing blue-green
waves roistering with the rocks
never seen such seeming playfulness
dazzling phosphorescence
make you think of Rimbaud
"recovered, what? eternity, the sun mating with sea"

and far out as you see some of the bigger ones
coming together, gathering themselves up
so inviting and beautiful
you could lay on their bosom
for a fraction of time
before they threw you on the beach
or the black rocks
smothered you under
lunging over the breakwaters and jagged promontories
charging up the beach with their brilliant manes
and then still others
coalescing somewhere in the distance
beyond your ken
only a slight arrythmia of conjunctive events
building, coming
from the mysterious deep

sleepers
beware

sneezing

you have a whole fits of it
veritable explosions one after the other
your face erupting
blowing snot and spit across the room
or against the furniture
sometimes you've got to go around
with some tissue paper and wipe it off

it's inherited and runs in the family
your mother has similar moments
brought on, you theorize
by food
and especially by coffee
sunlight
motes of dust
or seemingly nothing at all
you surmise it's caused by toxins or pollutants

your friend likes them he says
because they're like orgasms
one day only slightly after you've had an orgasm
you start to sneeze
and the juxtaposition in time
allows you some comparative judgment
and voila! some instinct tells you he's right
blowing off at both ends you wonder?
but still you can't stand sneezing
this being totally out of control
momentarily blinded while driving
like fits of vomiting only through the nose
for you it's not just once
each time there's a series, four to six
with ten or twenty second intervals
in which the pressure irritatingly builds up
after which each time you curse wholeheartedly

but what, you ask yourself, if it's
your body's way of expelling pollutants
of which there are always more and more
and if you didn't sneeze
you'd die or grow ill even sooner
this strange possibility that something you don't like

is helping you out somewhat
like everything else
confoundedly absurd
maybe in the end
when they've got you lined up against the wall
you'll start to sneeze
as though your body were trying to expel
the interlocking series of events and substances
which led you to this point
and you'll either miss the last few seconds of your life
or confuse the riflemen
by blowing off the black hood
and live a bit longer?

Sundays

going over to the VA
to see your old friend
now a toothless geezer
in for detox and arm broke
in two places, put a steel ball in
to hook it together again
i remind him it's his shooting arm
he could still play a mean game of horse at 65
9 of 10 from the corner
ask him if they give him anything good for the pain
"demerol"
is he dreaming, remembering or imagining?
"haldol"
that's for crazy people, no?
or maybe the d.t.s
go out to his old flat
to check the mail for some Social Security check
that's supposed to come
a bit nervous as i fish through the Mail Box
that must have served for him
and the people upstairs as well
nothing there of note
and no one questions my fiddling

back on the highway
you are remembering the one you were with
for a number of years
she and i would take off Sunday afternoons

cruise the old farm roads
make love where we could
in some hidden place
no one now to be with in the same way

and another
that ended in a lot of trouble
a literature teacher no less
you loved her as well
not that it mattered—
it never seems to
one time we were here on the outskirts
stopped at a Chinese grocery
bought a can of chicory coffee
too bitter for her
although that's what they drank in the South
but the bitter flavour suited you
and a good thing when you think of it

i stop there, and an old Chinese clerk
who can barely understand me
finally hunts it down
in a different place now
like retrieving a memory

coming back in
think of the roads you traversed with the first
rambling all over up and down the countryside
there was still a gap
between the closing-in walls
and we made a run for it

now the gap
like the eye of a needle
shrinking
your eyes don't see that good anymore
still looking through
and what are the chances?

Previews of Coming Attractions

sitting there waiting for the film to begin
you hear the crowd modulating into an escapist chatter
that childlike note sounding from it
as if they're returning to some version
of that first imprinting
when they were five or six
began to slurp down cokes
gobble buttered popcorn

a kind of innocence in their tones
perhaps this is as light hearted as they get
but looking around
there seems a tremendous passivity exuding from them

but then you consider
why shouldn't they enjoy some escapist fantasy
when you think of what's waiting for them
in the street

now you sense the intense anticipatory pleasure
they're taking
even from the trailers
reminders of what's forbidden in the theatre
ads for soft drinks
a kind of foreplay

but no, it's not that they shouldn't indulge themselves
but that this is their meat more or less
from beginning to end—
that they don't break out

as for you
only the University series had much to offer
where the supposedly better foreign films play
you looked down on most of the nonsense
playing at the commercial theatres

you could remember back to when you saw your first real films
"Orfeo Negro," "The 7th Seal," "L'Ventura"
you had seen them when they first came out
at the Art Theatre across the tracks
in your first University Town

an awakening
the likes of which you never imagined

the old neo realists from Italy
Visconti, DeSica, Antonioni
DeSantis and Fellini
the French, Resnais, Truffault
"Last Year," "Hiroshima," "Nacht und Nebel"
"400 Blows," "Shoot the Piano Player,"
even that goofball Godard
had made some first rate films
and Bergman, the Swedish master
you had cut your "eye teeth" on him
one masterpiece after another
for you, film's equivalent of Shakespeare
whom you never cared much for

and the Poles, when you were first back
from teaching in East Europe
they had some sort of retrospective on Wadja
in the middle of the week
"Ashes and Diamonds"
Poland just after the war, so grey and grainy
almost 50 years had passed
you even recognized a bit of the speech from the subtitles
this time it cut deeper into you
although it was perhaps the 6th or 7th time you had seen it
after the ticket-taker left
you were the only person in the auditorium
at a certain point it ran off the track
old print probably
the projectionist was apparently
out in the halls somewhere having a smoke
you had to hunt him down
he obligingly rewound it
to where it had gone astray
you watched the rest at this strange private showing
it puzzled you though why the young students
seemed to have no interest in this masterpiece

the Hungarians—
even the Russians sometimes slipped one through
Sanjat Ray with his "Apu" trilogy
there seemed some golden age in film

from the middle forties to the early eighties
after which something had gone out of it
not that there weren't good films still made
but that like writing, it was now mostly entertainment
rather than real expression

even the Americans had been forced
to put some reality into their films
so that there existed some discontinuous tradition of legitimate
   American films
even so, with most
you still felt that underneath all that violence and pretense
was a paucity of depth and feeling
that you could almost get at sometimes
by a kind of metaphorical unscrewing—
to such an extent that
at certain moments watching the new French films
which seemed to be trying
yet never succeeding in measuring up to their predecessors
it occurred to you
that perhaps you had wasted a large part of your life watching films
a dupe of modern society like so many others
your ancestors had lived their whole lives struggling to survive
and never once seen a film
forced by hardship to try to fathom the real things around them
what counted in the end was choice and action
we had been conned into this alienated kind of spectatorship
and now it was almost too late to recover from this decadence

or was it that you were old now
and it was dawning on you
how everything that seemed to mean something
gave out or came to a bad end?
people, art, friends, lovers, yourself

but then the film starts, an English comedy
one of the few
that doesn't insult your intelligence
well, if nothing else, the English can at least laugh
so for a few brief moments
we can imagine that we are some sort of more or less human beings
resuscitated from our fragmented, alienated, destroyed selves
into some semblance of humanity
we laugh out loud at this absurdist fooling about

that allows us a few legitimate sentimental moments
because it doesn't suppress the bleaker realities

that night at home before falling asleep
you find yourself asking some sort of half-formulated question
could it be that? . . . and you wonder what it is
but thinking about it more clearly
you sort out that it's some question of hope
for you or anything else—
remember an old friend long since bit the dust saying
"when you come up for air, breathe deeply"

over and over again you see them at the pool

over and again you see them at the pool
the somewhat retarded ones
they frolic about at the children's end
their caretakers watching out for them

and frequently it strikes you
that there seems no cunning in them
sometimes you feel more akin to them
than to the others

their tentative steps
into the jacuzzi
the hot water puzzles
and frightens them at first
how it works a bit beyond their ken,
once immersed though
they seem to grasp this laving warmth

but why then does even some average of intelligence
lead invariably to a cunning
and perhaps some mean-spiritedness as well

for you—to struggle your whole life
for a bare minimum of it
some sort of vulnerability
that had a terrible time growing a false face

you remember Primo Levi writing
that the best didn't survive the camps
the ones like him that lived to testify

blemished by some spurt of cunning
that carried them through in the end
these best and the "least" linking up?

looking back on the maelstrom of your life
it always amazes you
that you lived
the official world always posed against the individual—
for you it was only through your friends
giving a hand, more than a hand
even then you barely made it over the bar
some might say not even that
perhaps you were like some idiot savant
more idiot
but then when do you come full-blown
into silence, cunning, and exile?
exile the most profoundly true
cunning slow to develop
silence always the most problematic
how to get through to the others
like Pavese said
that's the most important thing, not so?
yet finally they force the muzzle of silence over our faces

most often the ones they bring here are fairly young
but now comes an older one
nearly my age
at first you almost don't "capiche"
that he's one of them
his face crusted over slightly with age
with that planet of the apes masklike quality almost normal
but then you see the troubled innocence and puzzlement in his eyes
and he keeps looking at you
as though recognizing a brother
yes — "mon frère
mon semblable"[1]

---

[1] mon frère, mon semblable: "my brother, my double" —Baudelaire

as though he were speaking in some Slavic perfective

as though he were speaking in some Slavic perfective
a spiritual Jehovah proclaiming "thy will be done"
but i walking down a flaming autumn street
realizing that i would live and die in the imperfective
even among the multi-hued leaves and mild autumn air
in the fragrant smokes of numerous leaf-burnings
 (can you die in the imperfective?
are you forced once and for all into the absolute?
or does your karma keep trembling and struggling
through various incarnations?)
always in an ongoing process
a movement toward
or a repeated action
to avail or no avail
or in the ability or lack
having done less well or better
in a thousand excruciating improvements and slidings-back
is this merely the human condition?
or some side of a great divide
in which we most stranded on the lesser side
and the few propelled by their singular qualities
into the perfect completion
where even to speak in the present
is to leap already into the future
as though to enter history by the front door
and be immediately recognized
and the vast perjority of us
mere enclitics[1] depending on the preceding
or post leading of multitudes
or will we some in a hopefully present tense
stand on our own in an existential infinitive
in all our imperfecticites
emblazon some approximate accomplishment
nonetheless
never the less
none-the-less

[1] enclitic: word connected to the preceding word, but not having an independent phonological status

for John Stack (1940-1998)

let yourself down through words
towards the silence
exhausted finally
by the whole of life

that's how it's arranged
to make you tired in the end
sleep
and then again sleep

even then
traces remain
of them
residues and stainings
of how they were
in some shutter between sleep and waking
the books with their crow's feet messages
the old ramblings

barely speak
find better to listen
sometimes to the words of others

take a walk down your river road
wobbling slightly
the little houses like some more ancient village
find remnants of what the river swallowed
only a few years ago
an old stoop, a few concrete stairs
with the metal railings still embedded
now like a stairway to the sky
that leaves off—
jumping off place
all that will be left of us

but this morning watch the dawn come again
in the greyness
the river so inscrutable
yet like some iconograph you are attempting to read

that you should live
while others not

a guilt
and an absurdity,
unless to remember

lights burning still
in a farmstead further on
forgot to turn them off, someone—
watch them reflected
in the dawn river

river at dawn

mist rising lightly above it
pinkening sky at the edge
old serpent river
crawls out of night
slithers along
ever so sluggish

threads of fog
phantasms
lifting there
drifting

as our lives
unreal struggle
grounded in anguish
watery weeds, dismal lees

this ground
linking us to others
even those gone past
around the bend of time and dissolution

but all of us finally
drifting alone
to river's end

where the great mouth
will spit us out
into the ocean of night
and darkness

old jack (for carol)

as you grow old
what to make of things becomes less clear sometimes
still the old arguments and counterarguments
you have your favorites
that you believe in or gamble on
but a troubling ambiguity has crept in as well

at other moments
the meaning of this strange drift of history
personal and public
seems overwhelmingly clear
but this too often passes in silence
as though so brutally bleak
or complex, you couldn't measure up
to truly speaking of it
and if you could, who would listen?

i remember Conroy[1]
the last time we saw him
in the intensive care of Moberly Hospital
already 90-something
he was lying naked under a sheet by himself
unable to speak
i had never seen anyone
look so totally vulnerable and anguished
so you and i made up for it
by speaking for him as it were
perhaps babbling away like two young idiots

he kept trying to find the words though
as if thoughts were still crowding
to form themselves into speech
his mouth working painfully   without result
finally   after an interminable struggle
in a kind of gravelly whisper
managed one simple sentence—
so this is what it comes to in the end
this man who had once written so powerfully

remembering a few years earlier
when you had taken your depression writers class
down to Northeastern Missouri to visit him

he took you out to the cemetery
near the old Monkey Nest Mine
that had claimed so many of his family
he talked of the curse of the Conroys
strange and violent deaths—
not mentioning this time
all their Marxist reasons

as we took our leave
he spoke more plaintively
with a sad poignant gesture of his hand
said "don't forget old jack"
we left him standing there among his dead
whom he soon would be joining

[1]Conroy: 1930's writer, author of "The Disinherited"

tree souls

if our close relatives
on the animal side
whales, chimpanzees, dogs, dolphins

on the plant side
we might be related to trees

perhaps we have two souls
one which travels, feels demonstrably
chooses, dances, the passionate train-journeying soul
whirlwind of discordant colouration
with Whitman in his "Song of the Open Road"
travels to the ends of the earth
leaving everything behind
for the sake of the journey
while retaining everything in microcosm

the other
stationary and rooted, almost trapped
speaks a quiet, somewhat abstract language
like the souls of trees
in which some instinctive nobility resides
it must endure enormous chunks of disaster and flood
hell-fire and damnation

catalepsis and transmogrification
children sometimes understand this tree soul
but as they grow up they are taught to forget

yet the stories trees would tell
if we could listen to them again
could hear them
seem to be of growing old
of friends cut down
the relationship of the forest
the land and the animals
of growing desuetude and loneliness
yet the tree endures
makes new friends
sings out again in whatever voice it can find
of some great longevity however short
but most of all
of the clarity and necessity of enduring

unexpected voices penetrate us
interpret for us these trees

if we could decipher
the magic knife stuck in the wood
quivering, singing this telepathic song

Pozor[1]

life is mainly a blockade
sea-quarantines
check points
night border crossings
internments

we seek to enter
the heart of the country

"regret to inform you . . .
. . .. given the prevailing conditions . . .
not at this time . . .
nor in the foreseeable future . . . "
"so goodbye sleepyhead
and remember, don't smoke in bed"

[1]Pozor: danger, watch out (Czech)

Time (for Kjell Askildsen)

reading a Norwegian
some drama of a remote lighthouse-keeper's island
your memory opens back
and you recall lying on the floor in your late adolescence
the Sunday paper had an article on the death-bed remarks
of the literary and notable
you had asked your father what his might be
he replied without blinking
"now the farce is done"
and went back to his own perusal
surprised, you felt a kinship for him then
perhaps not so different after all

all these years later
without having properly thought of it for decades
you remember
only now, having almost lived your life
has more complex resonance
not less true
and a sort of muffled regret
only a faint and obscure hope to set against it
for then it was a protest and a premonition
at what since childhood had begun to swallow you up—
you hadn't lived through the clattering and wrenching years
which, when they let you up for air,
having gained some strength and purpose,
you struggled it to a standstill
only for brief moments

but thinking of it now
good for a rueful smile
and a bleak sense of how it rings

unemployment office

you can't remember . . . was it fifteen years ago?
they put you on to some yard work . . . for half a day
other than that you only come for unemployment
that is compensation   to shoot an angle
but in the last few years
you managed to hook on once out of five
the first time you had made too much in your main quarter
the next what you were paid wasn't actually work money
that is wages, but some temporary grant fund
after that too little in your second quarter
then leaving insured work for uninsured
it blurs then into all the times you've fought them
for some meagre subsistence
you used to win more often
now the various exclusionary rules multiply
into a blank wall with little entrance
the paper and radio say lowest unemployment in years
yet if less actually get their benefits
then fewer are on the rolls as statistics
but today the office is jam-packed
certainly no middle or upper-class people
strictly a slave mart
a stolid look
impassive you would say?
expressionlessly stoic
preserving themselves somehow
through the battering of the years . . . but you wonder
what's really left of them
a darker darkness under the eyes of a black woman
if they talk at all it's with subdued voices
each alone here with the system
hardly any solidarity left in them
except some remnant that might be dug up one day
the state workers not as bad as in previous years
they don't scream at you any more
nor say that you should be taken out behind the building
and have the shit beat out of you
they must have sent them to sensitivity training
or some were sued and lost their jobs
there's a coldness here though
the rocky countenances

of those who devised or administer all this—
to see these shuffling figures
covered over to varying degrees
with some shadow or caul of human darkness
their eyes seemingly only a few degrees less cold
than the system itself and its representatives
"don't give a fuck" you hear a black man saying further back
some of the workers know you at this point
sometimes they seem almost human
at worst only somewhat contemptuous and antagonistic
at best neutral or maybe faintly sympathetic
it's the system itself which freezes us into human blanks
filtering, filtering us out
screening, as from behind a screen
caught between the bosses, landlord, bureaucrats, falling wages
the numbers which are always against you
with no real chance of using your skills
and being fairly compensated—
when you look into the eyes of the duffer
who's at the front desk
—like some old turnkey eking out his days
you know you're one of the condemned

some young kid who seems to know you
smiles a goofy smile as you're leaving
yeah kid, we're some of the dark ones alright
get ready for it
the long uphill pull till you croak off
old Camus' Sisphus our pard

food give-away

coming here again as i have for years
i notice the bodies of the poor
a few shriveled and shrunken
others blown-up and bulged out
poverty takes their bodies and twists them on a rack
in the end they are all out of proportion

yet these bodies seem so familiar
like the back of your hand
as if we were born into a distorted world
and in this world of distoring forces and mirrors
all this was inevitable

i am instructed by these poor
by the physiognomies
by their physiques
their few spare words
the planes of light
made by these misshapen figures
cut into me like a sculptor's chisel

in your mind's eye
you see them in their final "grotesquerie"
but to you
they are whole
brought back to their virginal oak

for Yoga Barbara

wends her way over in the chess cafe
would like to vote for Nader, she says
tells me he will be speaking here today in our town
but she fears that if Gore is beaten
Bush would take things back to the dark ages
and as she says "ruin all our lives"
but, i say to her, our lives are ruined already . . .
so she might as well go ahead
and listen to her conscience

returning to the chess game
a kind of beautiful absurdity
hammering away on this abstract anvil
to reach a moment of consciousness

the day before the election
after hearing that most of my friends were voting for Nader
i decide to vote for Gore
to sort of balance things out
and since they say it's neck and neck

actually the most real thing
would be not to vote at all
because none of this will free us from our oppression

but you've got to have some sort of strategy
however absurd or rear guard an action
amidst such monstrous realities

late on election night in the early hours
still half asleep
i hear that Bush has won . . .
and a great sadness comes over me
i almost weep
the people have been beaten again
tried to . . . rise up . . . make their small choice count for something
but . . . could not
dark times . . . many will suffer
some not live

winter flies

a small group
still crawl slowly up the window pane
of the old Iowa farm house,
winter sun outlines their passage
as though ascending some invisible meridian
the bodies of their mates
strew the window ledge

although vexing, with their throbbing buzzing
you think, "let them live
the winter will do them in
soon enough
even though they are inside,
and if one survives till spring . . . ?"
consider the last few thoughts
or realizations that even a fly must have
to complete its life

just some other god
might be watching you
and say "he'll do himself in
given half a chance."
or "conditions will finally become too much."
and string you out
a little longer

Kant, Kyrgystan

standing at the edge of a playground in Central Asia
thinking of my father's coming death,
the beaten earth in front of me
scuffed, denuded , trampled
frozen, rained on, thawed
dusty candy wrappers, equipment twisted, rusted, decrepit—
the pounded earth,
rekicked and scuffed anew
footfalls of the generations
empty now—abandoned
not a quiver

suddenly comes to life, again teeming, populated in my imagining
by the poor Turkic-karakyrgysz and Illinoisians
mingling somehow in their youthful gymnastic vigours
feeling my father's spirit
when he was a young coach
walking among them, urging on, pointing out
lapses of technique and movement
giving guidance, cutting a perfect path, moulding,
speaking to them
making his way through the multitudes of attempting athletes
a word here, a gesture there
aiding, calling to account
cutting through the their flawed movements like a surgeon
lighting up their efforts
until, diminished at the end, he disappears
and they too fade out
taken off by the grinding wheels of history—
the playground now again quiet, still
the baking afternoon sun
no one left in my strange reverie
something between hallucination and deliberate willing

choke back what rises in my throat
having seen something of his youthful spirit
re-embodied to his prime,
then silence—
of absence
loss—
intimations of what must come

slow learners

our whole life a struggle
to learn even the most elementary things
... to enter into these mysteries
in order to ascertain

lucky we come part way
but always it seems
with some considerable distance still to go

over and again
we are forced to try to straighten out
a disproportionateness
which seems embedded in the fabric
right from the beginning
making everything crooked

as to special subject matters
we might touch upon a few of these
before they are snatched away
by some abrupt termination

when we try to measure our progress against that of others
we find many ahead of us,
to be the dark horse moving up on the outside
in a few frames
the best we can hope for

and if we learn one thing
there is always another we have neglected
in its wake

by the time
we are beginning to understand
a few basic and most important things
and we might be capable of returning
something to life
something else
comes tapping, insistently
as in the old Norwegian folktale
a bird pecking at the window to get in

audience

the laughter that comes out of them
is like canned laughter
that was put into them
years ago, when they were children
it comes out inappropriately
at any slight incongruity
implying things are funnier than they are
hearing it
your instinct is to never laugh again

it goes on and on
a laugh track that never ends
but then you forget about them
and your own natural laughter comes back
until one day you hear them again somewhere
that nervous deracinated titter

you consider that someday they will sober up and grow silent
or else a savage hilarity will finally burst out of them
demented hyenas
screech owl spooking the night wood, tuning his mating call
torrent of bitter and coruscating mockery
shuddering and barking
until it becomes hysteria and weeping
and then finds silence once more

roads and the night

roads and the night
more and more snow
coming at an oblique drifting-down angle
following Emily's directive to "make it slant" [1]
driving into the origin of it,
heading from whence it came
Kansas, Dakotas, the true north?
river to the west frozen, drifted over—
Mr. Blizz—àrd out in the yard
semi come barreling down the narrow blacktop
miles from any city   a demon from hell
balling the jack from what industrial subworld
where headed? _____into the night further and further
to the end of night

the drifts erupting
blowing over the road
some miragy white floor shifting under us
"dancing in the stroboscopic dark"
weird tango of my thoughts—
lemmings pulverized into white dust
heading still for the sea
agitated snow, up and migrating on its own—
straining now, straining
to still be able to see the yellow line
where the road's center might be

pulling up to the small town
pulling close
the frigid luminescence glittering **absolut**
light from a long-dead star
that once held a promise,
but no more

turning through the drifts
banging through them, the wheels shifting unpredictably
the road itself cut out of a larger drift
finally the little relay station for electric,
transformers outlined in the metallic light
something men had left on the moon

to the end
the end of night
some other realm
some further place
half mile more
then sleep and dream
of being with the coyotes under a great drift
huddled together fur on skin, skin on fur
varmints all
to sleep in the bosom of grandfather night

[1] "make it slant": Emily Dickinson

Nerval

reading Nerval again
it's been years, you think
and you never read him properly
as you did Rimbaud, Verlaine, Baudelaire, Artaud

was he a bit of a pale classicist?
or did the translator pick the excessively
artsy-fartsy Parnassian poems over the others?
you resolve to go back and read his entire "oeuvre"
for in bygone years
you were quite struck by all these "poétes maudits"[1]

at twilight, wandering the city
in the fog and rain
the city in which your life
had darkened and silted up
you understood
how it would be quite natural
to hang yourself, as he did
from one of those tall, lugubrious, hanging down
over-shedding lamp-posts

[1] poétes maudits: "Damned Poets" (French)

flight

everything must be negotiated
and you think of the painful process
taking the course of the years,
in which all the permissions and refusals
make the pattern of circuitry
like transistor junctions forking and deciding

even death will have to be negotiated
the ins and outs of it
in a last teetering

worse when nothing
can be negotiated
you are up against the wall
the final impasse

even in prison you had to go on negotiating
under the terrible dense pressure,

we have to negotiate
because we are not free,
what if one day nothing need be said
and you simply did what had to be done?

—if there were some natural understanding between us?
impossible

yet, in this damnable world
there are brief moments
which give us the idea
of how it might be done

metaphysical questions

when i was a child
i went with my father one day to visit a friend of his;
in the friend's living room there was a saying
hung on the wall in a frame
"vhy iz zar so many more
horses azzes
zan horses?"
this quandary puzzled me
i pictured horses cut in two standing around
as in a comic strip
"but what about the front of the horse?"
i asked myself

now, years later it comes back in different ways
the comic and the sad
the bitter and the ridiculous
no doubt there are still too many cut up horses
but the solution continues to elude us . . .
similar to the problem of the physicist,
when he tired of leptons and quarks
"why are there more assholes than . . . ?"

these quandaries will plague us right up to the grave
will make us laugh and cry and rave with anger
and they will not be solved in our lifetime

reading your own poems again

reading your own poems again
it finally becomes clear
how it cuts two ways and the sense of it
the worst reason is for vanity's sake
this fault which seems so unshakable
but, in the end
flows into the common cesspool of myriad human flaws
the better part
is that reading your own words
you're reminded again
of who you are
all of it written against the grain
and although so much of it
full of sadness and pessimism
this was the better part of you
and at whatever stage
of this indeterminate struggle to mean something
to go forward no matter
for against this
was always your own society
fostering, building within its collective psyche
a vast amnesia of individuals
whatever might have been unique and different
this always to be crushed and forgotten
telling you that you were never anything
and never would be anyone
this jackhammer on our whole lives
so that whoever we might have been
obliterated to a pulp
almost forgotten even by ourselves
so that we are forced to struggle
to even remember ourselves
aside from the anonymous pieces of shit
that they regard us as
so for us all
try to be kind to that best different part
stand up for your own struggles
even though forced to the margins and interstices
so that when they come with their bulldozers
to push us into a mass grave
we hadn't forgotten
in that last instant
that we stood up and were ourselves

American night

at night
in the solitude of my wanderings
i am often given pause
in those remote quiet neighborhoods

at each streetlight
i am tempted
to kneel and pray
at the very center of those yellow cones of light

yet only a nanobyte of resistance
is necessary to restrain myself
the knees aren't much good from old injuries
one might get run over by a car

and you would have to ask yourself
what god seen or unseen would you beseech?
certainly not
the god of electricity

yet the sense persists
like a kind of "idée fixée"
to make this naked desperate plea
for yourself? for others?
a gesture beyond absurdity?
down the darkened lonely streets
one   by one
like stations of the cross

the trouble with most people

"the trouble with most people
is that they can't follow directions," she said

"they can't do the simplest thing

can they stop at a stop sign, no they can't"

"i've seen people stop at a stop sign," he said

"the simplest forms, they fuck them up
they can't organize what's necessary"

"maybe they don't want to follow directions"

"how are you going to organize our complex rigamarole of
    societies
if they can't follow directions?"

"maybe they're tired of following directions"

"i'd have given you an F, absolutely
without thinking twice"

"if you create a society in which all that is asked or required
of people is that they follow directions
then?

if they're an actual real functioning part of society
they wouldn't need to assume their computer chip
function by following these endless directions"

"ignorance of the law is no excuse"

"but isn't that why Kafka wrote his stories?
because the law is this massive unknowable thing
growing exponentially in unforeseeable ways
and we under it ruled inexorably"

"if they would just learn to follow directions
it would be so much simpler"

"back when i tutored my Vietnamese boat gal
she was an elementary ed student, i didn't know
anything about it, but naturally that didn't stop me
from tutoring her—i finally figured out, that in education
the main thing is sorting out what the teacher wants you to do

in other words, deciphering her directions, the tasks themselves
were mostly busy work

and so the prospective teacher gets used
to focusing her main concentration
on the directions of her superior
and this of course becomes the model
for her own instruction"

"isn't that why people are penalized and stigmatized
because they don't follow even the most minimal directions?"

"maybe it starts to dawn on them they'll lose either way
as they say in German 'es ist ganz egal' " [1]

[1]Es ist ganz egal: it's all the same

at night

at night
the train, shunting cars in the yard,
its wheels grinding and screeching against the rails
cries out for us
better than we ourselves could
having in some ways
grown nearly mute

a long continuous yowl of a rasping cry
as though expressing
a rending song
of our own articulation

we will live again

your mother
her memory slipping and mental powers failing
has resurrected the dead
claims that she is at her mother's house
rather than her own
but puzzles "i haven't seen her
yet though"
as if it were exceedingly strange
to be there in her mother's domicile
and yet not seen her, still nevertheless
retaining some sense of checking things out
with her faculties

shuddering at the mind's disintegrations
by what right are such things visited upon us?
remembering your friend's account
of taking care of his daddy during his last days
he had resurrected his whole family
as though they all still lived in some twilight zone together
finally one day
after his father had blethered on about them for weeks
your friend in a moment of frustration lost his temper
"don't you understand," he said, "that they're all fucking well
   dead"
his father just blinked at him with pained incomprehension
and surprise

you remember years ago
the one time you had seen their family all together
at some rare and unique reunion
it was like watching "Long Day's Journey into Night"
how they tormented one another

all this gives added impulse
to live now
without holding back
however we twist around each other
in some dance of mutual incomprehension

for Wanda

ten years ago
i went to an anarchist meeting in the twin cities
the oldest person there
was a woman a few years older than me, maybe 54 or 5
greying, an intellectual, she published a newsleter
on the evils of television
she considered it a diabolical addiction like some drugs
something of a mover and shaker
we spent some time together hanging out
she tried to tell me what it was like
getting older as a woman
she said the problem was
that people didn't see you anymore
you began to disappear, first the hands
then the legs, an arm
the midriff . . . i think she was dramatizing
then you were gone
you were invisible . . . lost in the mists
the last bit to go, she maintained
were the breasts, after everything else had dropped away
sometimes they still saw the tits coming toward them
like headlights in the fog
i would have thought it was the ass
but how would i know?
but then she said, "they" began to crumple and sag
and there's nothing left of you worth seeing
just men? i asked, or women too?
certainly men, but a lot of women as well, she answered
it's as though they know you're no longer in the running
you have no ascertanable value in the reality of flesh
older women had told her the same
she had discussed it with her girl friends
apparently some of them, when they first experienced
their invisibility it was like a blow, a blow to the body
a few had serious depression, went into a tailspin
what about the face, i said
it sort of expresses the character
well, of course, sometimes they have to see your face
but often, without a body, you don't have a face
the death knell, she said, is when they start to call you "maam"

i took what she said

as the handwriting on the wall
the years pass and i begin to experience it as well
a kind of selective blindness or blotting out
women certainly, but a lot of men as well
there are less "serious" conversations with women
because there's "nothing" these conversations could lead to
your old lover on the other side of the country

tells you on the phone that her flesh withers
from lack of touch
you'd think we invisible ones could help each other out
but maybe once you've been invalidated
you don't have the strength
to show much compassion for the others
or maybe some part of us has the same "view" as the majority
if only you could still find one of the living flesh

it's been a long time now since you've found a lover
some days your flesh creeps with loneliness
tonight you watch the moon rising in the spring night
and the sap seems to rise in you as well
for a week you've felt a desperate sense
of having to find someone
confirming McCuller's "the heart is a lonely hunter"
your soul aches with a bemused deprivation
and you remember that old gal who told you the skinny
the way it was

and some young girl, a hard luck case
from years ago when you lived in New York
you heard her voice across the air shaft on a hot summer's night
telling somebody "he didn't love me at all, he didn't care for me
he just wanted to get into my pants"
then stifling a sob
over and again like a litany

and then even as everything finally quieted down
and you sat by the window
breathing in the stench
of hot night air
it seemed you could still almost hear
the eerie echo
or faint harmonic of her sad cry
falling through that deep shaft
to the bottom of our blackened hearts

a hard row to hoe (for Rick)

you and your old pal Joe
were doing strawberries
hoeing weeds out the rows
your radiator had blown in NY
and from then on you were riding the dog
the old man who owned the orchard had hired you back
you had done the apple harvest ten years before
he had always treated you fairly
it was his son, the foreman
who was the asshole
troubled you the first time
mocked you when you were a little lame
scrambling around in the tops of tall apple trees cutting the suckers
but already in your 40's not as agile
and now again gave you a few dirty looks
there was a kind of arrogance to him
that must have come from growing up a boss
you had told them that you might only
be able to work a week or ten days
because you were trying to arrange
transport back to the midwest
to resume your old life
how long you could work
was contingent on what you could sort out

when you had to go after a week or so
they seemed to accept it prima facie
someone was going to sell you another used Renault 18i
for $400
a piece of luck
but the deal fell through
so you had to take the greyhound back
you had to be there for the beginning of school
to start tutoring
when you got back you tried to collect another few weeks of
    unemployment
because the University only paid a piece-rate hourly wage
you started with one student for one to two hours a week
and then two . . . etc. until you built up
to ten or fifteen of them
the unemployment office of course had to contact
the orchard in Vermont, and they protested

saying that you had left there of your own volition
and so didn't deserve it
even though it didn't come from any of their money
being based on previous work in your own state
but as a matter of principle—
but what principle and whose?

you couldn't make the hearing
but submitted your argument in writing
maintaining that at some point
you had to leave that job which was only temporary
to resume your old one in the town in which you actually lived
naturally you lost
but you asked for a copy of the tape they made of the hearing
so here you are some months later finally listening to it
hearing the arrogance ooze from the foreman's voice
as it was recorded over the telephone
and the unemployment guy kissing his ass
in some old boy's hot-shot embrace
the funny thing is that i probably
still have that tape in some dusty box
of old manuscripts and papers
and in just such a way
you come to know on which side your bread isn't buttered

but you consider
that it's almost better
to make the fight and lose
because then you start to understand how it works
and why that loss was already in the cards
and how it's stacked up against you
and why it's going to be a hard row to hoe
but for you to take it up then consciously as a struggle
and one day maybe you'll finally shove that hoe
right up their ass
the privileged and the powerful
will shake their heads
and ponder the bitterness and anger
that bore down on them
and never grasp anything except that the poor
are monstrous, subhuman, and insane
and even then years later die without ever understanding
that they have lived their whole lives as assholes
with not even the briefest of inklings

blind alleys

each blind alley
is like a through road
for a short distance

not having reached the end of it
there is no difference
at that point,
or do we feel the narrowing
of the passage?

at least in our life's experience
we do not have to return
backwards all the way
to the entrance
there is simply dead space
then a new road begins
to take shape
however fragmentary

in Danish it is called "Blind Vej"
in life all blind ways
lead on to the headwaters or mouth
like many roads, narrow and crooked
or great and clear
run together
stippled by the scars
of our cramped choices

we try to grasp
the contours
of this journey
and almost manage it
by road's end

insomnia

can't sleep properly anymore
wake mid-night lie there in bed strung out
your life drifts back in some disintegrated phantasmagoria
memories all seem to have happened in the dark
as though everything took place at night
the people talk
like watching fish move their mouths in water
they say this—they say that
it always changes
what kind of blah-blah are they saying now?
they're becoming this
evolving that—some new hat
yet always it's the same old shit
moments of tenderness disintegrate like film that is tearing
the warmth drains out of the women
like oil from the crankcase
as soon as you pull the plug
they stare at you with those cold dead eyes—
friendships of youth gone by the wayside   more important things
    to do now
one memory takes the place of another
a changing game of solitaire

nonetheless these still have hopes
yet they seem vaguely troubled
feverish, confessing
proclaiming, talking in broken asides—cursing
their speech gathers slowly
like cosmic dust becoming planet and stars
a kind of invincible whispering slowly mounting up
they're rustling like dead leaves in a slight wind
they're having soliloquies with each other
nothing quite reaches to the other
they're stirred as well
what can you say—these are the people you loved
and you—you're one of them
you belong to them—this tribe of strangers
becoming even more strange
those that died early
probably better they didn't live to see it come to this
they're sleeping now in their own way—for good and just as well
if only
you could sleep again

no recourse but re-course

stumbled on each other in the grocery
unawares,
for the first time
in almost three years
her face seemed to have neither fear,
nor hate, nor masklike dissimulation
nor edginess
for three seconds
you saw the person you had loved
again, the better part
heard her voice saying hello, so clear and so much herself
and it came to you immediately, that for you at least
nothing had changed
all the trouble, a whirlwind nightmare of estrangement
had not altered the fundamental sense
for three days you pondered
how this could be
for in this life, so little is guaranteed
and so much destroyed as a matter of course
that this feeling could still be intact,
—you assumed it dead like a stump dug out of the ground—
seemed a revelation
then the unrequitedness came back
—old pain to grieve you
and the memory of all the trouble whirled about again
shit-storm of darkness, dead leaves, and detritus

after some weeks
as the experience began to be plowed under
by the passage of days
—something about the fidelity of feeling
made you think of Tolstoy,
and Dostoyevsky, whom you were now reading again

in the end despite the pain dug up
you reckoned it a good thing
not only that
but given the circumstances
perhaps the best thing
in some way that couldn't be fathomed

if we are destined to be these singular monads

moving through space alone,
each of us
must reckon up on his own
what lives, what dies, what remains

playing again at 60

nearly three months before your abilities came back
to some extent the old skill returned
the body knows what to do
even though it can't perform in the same way

today though you felt some absolute clockwork sense
the patterns spinning out so precise
as if measured with a caliper
a kind of almost physical "chess"
you'd seldom felt as a younger player
maybe dragging a little behind now
you trace the forms in a deeper groove
trying to stay with your man
in this game you've played for 50 years
everything moving so quickly
having to slide through three or four screens
in a matter of seconds
couldn't let him set up dead shot from the outside
Karl, your friend, who plays to keep up a struggle
against a fatal cancer which rather sooner than later—
will wash over him again in a wave
the body its own miracle coming back over and again
when we judge it decrepit and finished—
the patterns unfolding and crisscrossing
this exacting dance
navigating the turbulent flow and movement of it
sometimes showing up in the right "moment-space" to make the
 play
the years of experience fluxing though you
as if you played it in the womb
and before that among the stars

warming up you felt an absolute sense of surety
when your fade-away jumper off the opposite foot comes back
as if in some other life it was quite natural
to shoot left-handed, left-footed while moving away **and to the side**

today, instead of half a step behind a quarter
in the last game three for five and no mistakes
one of the baskets even a fast break
can't run so well any more and have a knee that is going
but you can still get off a few good steps
your legs finally loosening up
and not cramping again and again as when you first started back

the end of the game you look up
most of the players, no spring chickens themselves, younger and
    faster
but you feel equal to them in some way
a player among players
and one cannot ask for much more

pass foto

like fido or fou—
clearly a mug shot
shot after a lifetime of interrogation
"as to what you, asshole,
think you're doing in our screwed down world?"
sailor, what ship?
(from an old story by Tillie Olsen)
as though you mustov and undoubtedly
had the shit knocked outov you
47,000 times or been
hit in the head by an oar
at least 23 times
not so?
as though looking away
at the distance
or directly at you
both at once
or your grey beard
looking almost like an old woman's bush
"yours dbe grey too sonny
cracked as many nuts
as mine has"
or some shrugged off stevedore
with neither the sense
to come in out the rain,
or seen the whole crooked setup

so many times—
one eye and brow
tilted higher than the other
as though askance
or aslant the rest
beginning some last journey
toward the horizon—
shoulders taut and braced
ready for round 10
but almost indifferent to the outcome

they meant no harm

no screens on your windows
so the flies came in this summer
they would land on you like a kind of aircraft carrier
or maybe for a tasty bit of sweat

having no lover for two years
you joked with yourself
with more than a touch of bitterness
that they were the only ones now
willing to touch you

the little sons-of-bitches
would light-foot all over
whatever exposed flesh
they could find
until irritated beyond measure
by the endless creepy-crawlyness
of their landings
you'd say in your mind
that you were trying to live and let live
but if they didn't give you some space
you'd kill some of them

so you'd grab
a rolled-up magazine
and amidst awkward swattings
and too late WHAPS!
you'd finally get one of the little buggers

you'd see their poor crushed bodies

knocked to the floor
their brief season come to an untimely end
and you'd think that we all need
some kind of space
to live in, undisturbed and in peace
but lucky the ones to find such a haven
most living in various contested zones, as they do

you remembered visiting a friend
who lived right over the South Dakota line on a pig farm
the flies so thick around his little travel-trailer
it was hard to get a moment's peace
you went out and saw a hundred or so
bunched on some shit smeared on the side of a barn
killed most of them with one blow
but two or three hundred immediately landed
on the blood and carnage of their bodies
you crushed this new contingent with another blow
but it soon became too much for you
this one-man genocide
and besides, there seemed an infinite supply
ready to jump in the breach

now in late autumn
a few survivors buzz around
and you hope they will not trouble you too greatly
so that you can let them live out
their too brief span

for we are all crowding each other
in this strange life
and must, if we are to survive
reach across our alien differences
and make a connection with these other beings
who are with us in the total animal soup of time

blind in one eye and can't see out of the other

sometimes all you can see are the surfaces
but to understand truly
you've got to be able to see in to things
at least in some way
but too often you felt a kind of blank blindness
creeping over you, cataract caught from this society
as though even a fragment of insight
had become impossible

there's a blind man here in town
frequently you see him on street corners
stumbling around lost, unable to get his bearings
or calling out obstreperously
you know him slightly
his condition
makes him ask absurd questions of people
he thrusts himself into their privately held realms
angry and confused
demanding to know this or that
he's a big pain in the ass
but as you watch him
it occurs to you that
this is the kind of blind man you would be

sometimes you see him hitchhiking
in between fits of ranting and bellowing
would you hitchhike if you were blind?

when you were a child you'd close your eyes
and pretend for a while
you'd quickly run into things
stumble about
and have to cheat a bit
almost immediately
to keep from fucking yourself up good and proper

another blind man out in front of the court house
you had seen him around for years
but never spoken to him
you could see an intelligence in his face
some darkness coming from his sightless eyes

a somber beauty about him
his dog lay beside him in his harness
calm and assured
a real Mensch this blind man seemed
you both went in for the opening of court
you had to pay a fine for hitting another car
it was true, the fault had been yours
one of the few times where legal justice
made a grain of sense
he came to hear a woman plead to the charge of harassment
she wouldn't stop calling him on the phone
pleading her case
no great beauty, heavy set, and crippled to boot
still there was a sad look on her face
as though she had suffered
guilty she pled
was it that her soul, body
and voice weren't beautiful enough
she must have been in love with him

then you remember those human outcasts
who wander up to you in the street
selling key chains or little books outlining sign language
but you didn't have any use for any of it
occasionally you'd given him a quarter anyway
then it would occur to you
that this deaf man had to travel from town to town
a complete outcast, selling useless pieces of shit
just to make ends meet
you'd almost felt ashamed to be a human being

but why didn't we have any use
for this sign language of his?
why didn't in fact
we learn sign language in the 4th grade?
so that we'd all be connected
was it because we didn't give
that much of a fuck about it?

but then you'd seen the deaf together
signing their intricate dance of a language
rippling off a brilliant arpeggio of physical speech
a beauty beyond what can be created
by our poor babbledecock of sounds—

what secrecy of commentary
or in savage mimicry of our hearing world
your old friend had once taught in the school for the deaf
they showed him all the dirty words, so to speak
a carnifall of sexual and excretory puns

years ago in the 60's
after the sexual revolution had swept you up
we went to a party one night
you, your friend, and his wife, a dancer
you had already gone "menage à trois à quatre" with them
that night they brought along their blind friend
a woman who was a social worker for the blind
things started to liven up
we said to the others
let's strip dance naked
then maybe at the end have a love in
it was only early autumn indian summer on the prairie
all you had to do was drop your pants
no underwear
throw off your shoes no socks
for the women it went slower
the dancer was down to her panties and bra
you and your friend were already gyrating around
the blind girl though was much more meticulous
each piece taken off carefully
and stacked in a little neat pile

then you noticed the others hadn't really gone along
some down to their undershirts
taken off their shoes, a woman or two
standing in their slips like frozen mannequins
she "looked up" once half way through
as the music was drawing us in
almost as if she could see the beginning dancers
most stood watching us
as though we were
stone absolute freaks
aside from the music there seemed a silence

when we understood it wasn't going to go
there was a few seconds' lull
by the time you summoned the presence

to tell the blind girl
she had finally removed everything
without knowing
they were standing there watching her
with a blind cruelty which shown in their faces
she had a beautiful ass and pussy that stood right out at you
—so vulnerable in her naked sightlessness
we had to tell her then
they hadn't followed suit
and now we were going to put our clothes back on
and get the hell out of there

northern Manitoba

sometimes
no houses, farms
fields, animals or people
no billboards, no signs
no cars
except yours
only the road and you
bordered with these stunted trees
birches, aspens
a few conifers as you head east
flat land you always loved
a person might have half a chance on such land
but so far north, you don't know the bitterness of the winters here
but then far back to the horizon's edge a farm, some fields
wheat, oats, a crop that's densely yellow
and then one that has deep-blue flowers
traverse blue-green, wheat green, oat tan, deep yellow
a sign that says "fresh eggs in"
and a dirt road disappearing in the scrub
some cows resting in their shortened wooded glades
but then strangely over and over
signs even out here CRIME WATCHERS
or RURAL CRIME WATCH
your mind makes up some weird arrangement
of no one watching no one through periscoped reflected
    angles
who would there be to commit these crimes?
and who to observe and turn them in?
but do some "invisible ones" have their eyes trained on us,

or someone else?
rebellious Indian or Meti?
still disoriented from theft of land, destruction of culture,
    racism,
perhaps to them all life one enormous crime
or teenagers fallen out of the money-capitalist culture
acting out in this overmanaged life

but then cross an isthmus of Lake Manitoba
after passing a sign indicating a town "Reykjavik"
from Ashern East and South
you pull off for a historical marker
turns out this land was homesteaded by Eastern Icelanders
the head man commemorated, Sigurd Bjarnson
was skald and teacher
the plaque lists the plaits of all the settlers
the remains of Bjarson's homestead lying by this little river
which you don't find
the land in its almost chessboard, looking-glass quality
reminding you of parts of Denmark
stretches of Holland recovered from the sea
to the north over these trees less and less of us
good to know that human beings haven't yet overrun the
    whole earth
moving through these borderlands
you understand that traveling down these empty roads
can be quite lonely
how is it possible to start missing these beings almost
    immediately
upon first moving out of range of the dense massing of them
clearly a paradox

then abruptly pulled up short by Lake Winnipeg
it looks idyllic enough on this sunny day
you watch some "Scandinavian" teenagers swim off a boat
they seem happy to splash about
you skirt down the coast looking for a writer you once knew
    slightly
Valgardson, for whom Gimli, an old Icelandic town right
    on the beach
was his depicted world
he wrote of the bleak struggle of the Icelandic immigrant
    fisher-folk

the fall storms on the lake as they tried for the last haul
before the weather closed in on them
one of his books was called "God is not a Fish Inspector"
now Gimli with some sort of touristy gimmicky overlay
you wonder if anyone still fishes the lake
but walking around you find a few trawlers in drydock

heading south toward Selkirk and Winnipeg
it's clear you're back in "civilization" again
no doubt what to you was borderland
was small potatoes to the people living further north
you remember a guy you met in Cape Breton
who had worked Flin Flon[1] far up over by the Saskatchewan
   line
Flon, the Norwegian word for river?
no? case ending tacked on to Flod, for "flood"
the Flin river then?
but no river on the map
or Flon, being Icelandic for "oaf"
the whole shebang started by Flin, the oaf?
as good as Flintabbatey Flonatin
the grocer-adventurer, "first citizen"
of "The Sunless City"
the Cape Breton guy said it was seven thousand men and
   eight women
so you enter Winnipeg, one of the few cities you ever liked
the people actually friendly
but like many another only marginally registering your
   presence
still probably more important
you register its presence

---

[1]Flin Flon: Prospectors portaging near the Churchill River found a tattered copy of "The Sunless City" by Muddock. During long evenings they would read the novel, but never found out what became of Flintabbatey Flonatin because the last pages were missing. Later, on a lake which reminded them of Flin Flon's, they found an outcropping, staked a claim and named it.

American gridiron

at your school they didn't have a team
but playing sandlot
you had an instinct for it
to hit and be hit
especially to run with the ball
escape artist from the beginning
you had a natural sense to stutter-step
and cut back
leave them in the dust

finally there was a chance
to play organized ball in college
the people you played against
had at least 4 years experience on you
whatever your sense of it
it didn't measure up

you were 2nd or 3rd string fullback
play 31 was right up the middle
between right guard and center
32 the mirror image

scrimmaging against the first team
your wiry little quarterback would call that play
shove it in your guts as you ran past
the first string line
would be waiting with "open arms"
linebackers coming over the top and plugging the holes
you had to summon whatever waning instinct
might still be left . . .
the grunts and lunges
clunk and crunch of pad and helmet
mayhem of torsos, legs and arms, heads
lucky to make it to the line of scrimmage

one of the few times you got in a game
they put you in at end
for which you didn't know the plays
blindsided "tout suite"
went down like a ton of bricks

by the time it was over
you had lost whatever easy-going acceptance of rough-
   housing
knocked right out of you

that spring you took up tennis
a more civilized game
playing 3rd or 4th man
against other seedy teams on lost rain-soaked courts

but now, almost 40 years later, on native frost-bit mornings
when a storm is brewing up
and the fates are muttering their implacable curses,
you have strange memories and premonitions
of being in the 3-point stance
looking up the bore of some poor center
about to be massacred
the quarterback hunched against him as from the cold
starts to call the cadence
like quotations from the stock-market
the wind whistling mournfully up your arse,
still the 3rd string fullback
running on that line . . .
they are waiting for you
with out-stretched arms

global warming

or is it el nino? that's warming up these colder climes
these warm mild days in december
that come almost without interruption
you stop in a little park and bask awhile
as you make your way home
noticing the autumn leaves
that still hang tough on their trees
but there's also a little nip in the air
 (difference between autumn and a Japanese acrobat?)
with it though this strange new warmth
and it seems so gentle
so rife with a kind of tenderness
you cannot help smiling and laughing a little
nonetheless thinking of all the bad things
that will no doubt occur due to this greenhouse effect
the caps melting
the seas rising
flooding of coastal town and areas
disruption of various meteorological patterns
the deaths and dislocados
but for the poor up here in the north
this degenerative devolution
might mean a few more chances for awhile
a few less things closing in on them
before the "big bang"
and as you get up to leave
it suddenly strikes you
that this new pleasant warming
is like a drug perhaps
one of the worst no doubt
that floods for a moment
with some drowsy expansive warmth and embrace
leaves you nodding, chuckling
at some minor amusant
that in the end will perhaps do you in
but with a fatalism
that seems now almost complete
you cannot change any of it
why not accept then with a shrug and a smile
only a touch, a momentary remnant of irony

Illinois

years ago in the southern part
we'd go to a tavern in the ghetto
when such things were still possible,
a broken-down place called "Stumble Inn"
poor blacks a little under the weather
we too somewhat the worse for wear
dance a primitive stumble
groping for each other
feeling it in our bodies—loaded
one way or the other
everyone nearly equal

years later coming up the western side near the river
we hit a place
"Stagger Inn"
but only get a bite to eat

remembering childhood . . .
we lived near what they called "Bloody Williamson"
county that is
Ku Kluxers
labor trouble, gangsters out of East St. Louis
UMW and their bitter enemies the mine owners
with their Pinkerton goons and scabs
machine guns set up on top the tallest building in town
blacks sent to be strike-breakers
without knowing what they were getting into—
the orneriness
and cussedness
and feistiness of people in general

a few times passing through
we'd go past a certain tavern in Herrin
called "The Bloody Bucket"
where the miners drank
and fought and cut each other
it always gave me the shudders thinking of it

skirting the western edge along the rivers
through towns like Hardin
Kinderhook

Atlas
Mozier
keeping my eye on the wheat and corn fields, soybeans
that grow in the floodplain
of the Mississippi
between the bluffs
that rear up suddenly on the Western Shore
and on the Illinois side
drop back to a ridge of limestone
some miles in

this lip of land
like some lost bleak paradise
forgotten by nearly everyone
except for the people who live there
flashes on me gold and vermillion
yellow and brown
i could never have believed
or imagined
all the strange concurrences and perturbations

extra virgin

having a little more "bread" now
we reach for the "extra virgin" olive oil
yes, yes, cold pressed and all the rest
but more than that
it's time we are redeemed
made whole again
against this immutable corrosion
and so we reach
for some stored up sunshine's essence
ah! how good it could be
at least in our somewhat cracked psyches
to lave our worn out souls
in a bit of this extravirginity,
this green-golden fruited oil
from the "cradle of our civ"
dusky maiden and naiads
few of which we've ever seen
"only Euclid has looked on beauty bare," etc.

nonetheless we're forced to smile at the fabric of our self-deception
still attempting
in our fumbling and laughable way
to begin again
and rediscover at some too late state
some strange innocence
which has always eluded us
or perhaps that we once actually possessed
but is so deeply submerged now
that only some last estranged part of us
might know the whereabouts
of this far buried sunbathed mine
like a kingdom at the center of the earth

so we geezers, gaffers, duffers
mate with some sweet extra virgin
in the spawning ground
of our dreams' headwaters

watching a little group on the square

watching a little group on the square
these are the young "human scum" the businessmen want swept
    away
the bourgeoisie don't like them
they sit together on the edge of a raised flower bed quiet for a while
then one will make a remark
they all seem to understand   respond subtly with some small
    gesture or word
after a bit they lapse back into a silence
the fat ugly grotesque one
puts a ripped paper bag on his head like a hat
a kind of white "baker's chapeau"[1]
—they seem defeated
cast away here as on some invisible island
you sense abandonment in the eyes of one
thrown out
grasp the reason one can discern what's in his eyes
is that you have felt the same
a girl comes by
gives one of them some pocket change
as though she owed him
a few words are exchanged—
the fat one begins a sort of comic monologue
adjusting his torn "hat"
as if it helped him play some role
—reminds me of the old days
after getting high
when it was nearly over
we'd sit quietly with each other
at peace it seemed
it's like a Becket play
no doubt they are waiting for Godot
maybe these human scum are my sort of people
for a moment in any case
i am fond of them

[1] baker's chapeau: hat (French)

an apartment in the city of the dead

what good care they take of their dead here
flowers placed around the tombs
little votive candles lit feebly
in this grey blowing winter's day
you see the relatives in small straggling groups
arranging wreaths, or just standing there
quietly paying homage

as for me i could never quite get used to cities
but didn't like village life either, too narrow

all the Slovakian names sounding so somber and serious
the Slavic syllable "ova" tacked on to the end of the woman's
    surname
and sometimes a little picture somehow etched into the stone
showing the faces, a few died quite young, 19
or 27, you wondered how it had gone
a wild drunk and a car crash
lost love grieving to the end
or some absurd disease
even a pretty girl on one, her long hair

but as you walk to the end of the row
the cold biting your face
you consider if you'll meet some of your students
and they think you an intruder
on a kind of intimacy

you wonder what time the gates close here
as you wouldn't want to get caught—

you take note of the different family plots
with the name, such and such rodina, [1]
slowly filling up to a full house
finally two people you can identify with
an older red-eyed woman weeping openly at a recent grave
with flowers piled all around
and her crippled son staggering, lurching
his limbs palsied and askew
face somber and unreadable
his hands in serious pockets
as you leave you almost wish you were him

so you could stumble, shake, and wail
down the empty stupid streets of dying day
to give expression to this skewed life of unswallowable grief

but in actuality
he'll probably walk home
as best he can
being also a man learning to bear up
to all such things

[1]rodina: family (Slovak)

for Grace

i saw how the redneck-honyocks dressed up in their cowboy duds
pulled into the rodeo lot for the show,
you stood holding your sign protesting
the mistreatment of the animals
some sneered and snarled
gesticulated threateningly
outraged that you questioned their right
to whatever vicarious bestiality

i lay next to you as you wept for the 87 pigs
whose tongues had been cut out

i saw you separating your rescued cats from a fight
one gashed you deeply on the leg
you neither cried out nor complained

i witnessed you working with the rats
like some Pasteur or Madame Curie of the animals
laughing, playing with them, picking them up
moving from one cage to the other, in your element
speculating about this or that one
some were getting suspiciously fat
pregnant you thought
you hadn't separated them out early enough
someone had dumped them on your friend
and she secretly kept all 50 of them in her flat

you showed me the letters filled with hate
that were published in newspapers

from famous professors
raining down their scorn on you
for questioning their right to abuse animals

i was there when one or two people showed up
for lectures you had set up with out-of-state scientists
who questioned the animal model
for medical research

i saw the horror in your eyes
at the exotic animal auctions
for you it was the same as a slave block
you secretly photographed the cramped cages
and the fowls trussed up in them

i had to smile as you worried somewhat
about the cockroaches taking over your kitchen
you thought if you cleaned up the crumbs a little better . . .
you refused to let in the toxic sprayers
and couldn't bring yourself to kill one

on a frozen morning you and your friends
stood at the gate of the park
where the brave hunters were to be allowed to shoot tame deer
accusing them of murder

i listened to you speak your beautiful
drawn-out French on the telephone to France
speaking of "droits de animaux"[1]

late at night, exhausted, you pored over documents
finally extracted from the University Labs
looking for telltale revelations

i see you still
stanchion in the grey-passage
a thin girl in an old dress
you remain
against the obliterations of time

---

[1] droits de animaux: rights of animals (French)

for my father

another time's dime-store wind-up clock
late afternoon ticking
autumn's slanted light

old clock
bent clock
funny clock
fucked-out clock
—woke you with its tinny rattling
on inscrutable grey mornings
for terrible slave-jobs
that you worked to survive

clock which ticked your cheap time
through bare mattress and dust-mote
and Brownian movement afternoons—
as you grasped the living presence
of sundance moments

whose blank unreadable sun-dial face
kept improbably going
as you woke sweating
in the arms of your lover
who has now disappeared
into other dimensions of time

whose mechanism not built to last
throw-away clock
thrown away life
into the dustbins of history

clock, clock, clock
now reflecting, and giving back
(but also, not so? having taken by thievery
of our real subjective time)
absurdly and grotesquely
a few brief moments of time

your clock stops

crossing the Kattegat

back the other way
from the Jutland to Gothenburg
approaching the midnight sun
years come back blond and green

make the rounds at far remove
Puttgarten to Rodbyhavn
then later by another ferry
from Zealand to Ebeltoft
hitching south to Aarhus
where your old love once lived
the people extraordinary
they pick you up
and help you a little further on your way,
slept one night on the strand
at the city's edge
feeling the cold coming off the water

freighter cross our path
then passing behind
black hulk against the sheer incandescence
of the foam-churned sea

her sister told
that she never spoke of it
her sickness

you sat with some cast-off derelicts
outside a cafeteria in Fredrickshavn
found it good to sit with them in the sun

she showed a picture before the end
her face full of suffering
but smiling still a faded smile
as though looking down on us from some indescribable place
beautiful even then, with a touch of saintliness
and remote as Scandinavia itself
her hair gone by that time
a sad worn princess giving some kindness yet
the only look I had
into her later years

athwart our ferry some skerries
the bare rocks isolate
desolate
but on one
some grass, some earth
in the end she came back to her music
you thought of those last days—
of her listening and playing
after the cancer had deformed her beautiful breasts
then spread through her body

going north today
in the clear cool summer
feeling the wind coming off the sea
making for Aalborg
remembering those old dreams
in which you were always going north
struggling north, toward some sunlit, high-up plateau
on which you would find her again
speak to her in some meta-language
of silence and love
about the lost years, the lost people

now the seagulls come from Sweden
screeching, calling, diving, sailing
their bleak cries

sitting in the evening
eating supper with her mother and sister
together you'd talked up a storm
as though undiminished by a sadness
that creeps in from time to time
her father dead these twelve years
husband and son visit only at Christmas and Easter
family nearly whittled down to these survivors
they treated you like some long lost relative
washed up by the tide
their warmth touched and amazed
you and her mother recognized each other
in the train station
after so many years
joked with her sister
"like Halley's comet, every 27 years
by the next time we'll all be dead"

made the rounds you had to make
the ones left only for you
with their help
completed what couldn't be explained

this leave-taking morning
you considered visiting her grave
speaking to something of her
but—too vulnerable
—a torrent of sadness shatter you
put it off
till some still further time
the inner clock—time to go
and this sense gives a balance
perhaps make-believe
that lets you live between the tollings

slowly edging in to Göteborg harbour
city limit on the rocks
strange empty dream
city of your exiled friends
of darkening moats
and extraneros [1] of many coats,
a blond girl standing beside an empty idling taxi
gives you directions to Majorna [2]
but says in perfect English
and with a strange vehemence
"but i am not the taxi driver you know"
"yes," you mumble to your self, starting off
up the hill following the sparvagn [3] tracks
"you are not the taxi ferry no doubt"

remember years ago you dreamed of her
went to the land of the dead
she was there
took your hand, said not to be afraid
was just as she always was
told you that
it was alright

[1] extranero: stranger, foreigner (Spanish)
[2] Majorna: a district of Göteborg
[3] sparvagn: streetcar (Svensk)

Dingleberry (for Meridel)

return to the old swimming hole out amidst pasture and meadow
fondly remember how we laughed and climbed over the gate
which read NO TRESPASSING NO SWIMMING...
no this no that no everything

the beginning of the end came
when they leased it to a stone quarrying company
who drained most of the water by digging a drainage ditch
to a close-by stream—
devastating the ecosystem—
in order to quarry out rock for road gravel from just one end

but now finally bulldozed, whole hills
knocked down, decades of trees
stripped hillsides, blocked streams, new dirt mountains
made a long road for the rich who will soon move in
it's like coming on the scene of a crime
if it had been humans the victims of genocide
they would have pushed them into a mass grave and covered it up
but with trees, earth, animals
they don't bother to hide it
instead make further threats TRESPASSERS WILL BE
    PROSECUTED

you have to climb over giant brushpiles of tree corpses
your old personal tree as well, that you used to hug and commune
    with
smashed and murdered
you take hold of some broken off limbs
which lie close to where it was
to keep solidarity with whatever bits and fragments

make your way apprehensively through the ruined landscape—
feeling that any moment the criminals may return
to hold you before collaborator judges and justices of the pieces
because you realize that all this is probably perfectly legal
the rich and powerful, the developers,
have no doubt prepared the way
reminding you again
that the most serious criminals are the legal ones
with this or that state or capitalist justification

not even the cows left
whom you always had to watch out for when they were with calf
they'd get a snootful and chase you down the road
the dried up streambed bank where you'd had acid memories
and learned to pray
ripped from the ground and obliterated—
moving along a path still there
skirts the very cliff-edge overlooking the dried up basin
look out over it all
        sacrilege and horror
follow the path like a thread not yet torn out of the fabric
the trees that are still left
this crime held within their silence
they the lone witnesses who must sustain continuity

you mumble an incoherent prayer
but think that the spirits, which before, you were always skeptical of
will understand
hope with a flood of desperation that there have to be spirits
to hold some vestige intact

the story the old fisherman who fished here told:
in the 19th century the first settler residents of the land were the
    Dingleberries
a white man and an Indian woman who lived by hunting and
    trapping
caught bear, wolf, fox, beaver
when she died they wouldn't bury her in the city cemetery
because of her being Indian
so the relatives planted her out here on the land
we used to search for her grave
but never found it,
marker lost to the passage of time?

you used to ponder on the old woman,
as though she might be some sort of spirit of place
when you'd feel most alien to the people in the town or they to you
you'd think: "bury me with old Mrs. D"
remember telling your old gal Schnu
to put you here or spread your ash

now the Indian will be the sole representative
crumbled pieces of something left

old woman dingle of the berry
call up coyotes to yip at dusk in back hollows
shiver the timbers of the rich in their locked houses
till they too
pass under the earth
and are redeemed